BAD OMENS

WITCHES OF PALMETTO POINT BOOK 9

WENDY WANG

CHAPTER 1

Forty-two days.

Forty-two days had passed since Charlie Payne realized she could no longer see the dead. No longer sense other's thoughts. No longer see glimpses of the past or dreams of the future.

Charlie sat in her cousin's café and closed her eyes. She brought her coffee cup to her lips, her fourth cup so far that day. The steam from the sweet milky concoction warmed her face, and she breathed it in. She didn't know how much longer she could keep this secret or keep faking to her family that everything was just fine.

Forever?

That wasn't going to happen, but she'd hold out as long as she could. What sort of psychic witch was she if she was no longer psychic? She shook off the thought and opened her eyes and looked out the big-paned window onto the dark, empty street. She hoped she'd find her boyfriend Tom Sharon approaching the restaurant, but she only saw dead leaves swirling along the sidewalk.

A cold wind rattled the front window of the café, and there was still no sign of him outside. He was late. Again. The third time in as many weeks.

"You look like you're a million miles away," a familiar voice said. Charlie glanced up to find her aunt, Evangeline standing next to the table. The dark red scarf wrapped around her aunt's neck set off the silver of her long straight hair.

"I didn't realize you were still here," Charlie said.

"I had to catch up on the books. Jen hates anything to do with math, so it falls on me."

"Perils of being partners in a business with Jen." Charlie gave her aunt a wry smile.

"Indeed. May I sit?" Evangeline gestured to the chair across from Charlie.

"Of course." Charlie straightened up in her chair and put her cup on the table. She glanced at her watch.

Evangeline draped her navy peacoat over the back of the chair and took a seat. "Are you expecting someone?"

"Tom," Charlie said.

"We've missed seeing him at Friday night dinners," Evangeline said. Charlie glanced away, afraid of what might come next. Afraid of her aunt's steady, curious gaze.

"He's had to work a lot," Charlie said.

"We've missed you, too."

"I've had to work a lot, too." Charlie spun her cup in her fingers.

"I know, but I miss talking to you. Seems like the only time I hear from you is when you text me about Evan."

"I know. I'm sorry," Charlie started then fell silent.

Evangeline folded her hands together and rested her chin on top of them. Her sapphire blue eyes glittered in the light. Her piercing stare settled on Charlie's face.

"Evan loves his lessons with you," Charlie said, trying hard to change the subject.

"He's a smart boy. Maybe too smart for his own good," Evangeline said with a proud grin. "He's a natural-born witch, just like his mama."

"He'll be happy to hear that." Charlie sipped her coffee. "So, is there anything new going on?"

Her aunt cocked her head slightly and narrowed her eyes. Her crow's feet spread like a dark spider's web, and she said, "Same old, same old." Evangeline adjusted her red scarf. "What about you? It sounds like your new job is keeping you extra busy. Do you still like it?"

"I do." Charlie's smile faded at the hollowness of the words. "I just had my first real arrest; I mean that was all mine. A ring of witches was selling faulty spells to the general public."

"Congratulations," Evangeline said.

"Thanks."

Evangeline nodded. "I guess there will always be scammers."

"Uh-huh." Charlie's cheeks heated. Did her aunt think she was a scammer? At times like this, she missed her gifts the most. It drove her crazy, not having some sense of other people's thoughts.

The bell over the door rang, and a burst of cold air rushed into the cozy dining room of the restaurant. Several patrons glanced at the door and shivered. Charlie wasn't sure if the collective shivers were because of the cold, or because Tom Sharon was a reaper. Tom waved with one hand and unwrapped the striped wool scarf around his neck with the other.

Charlie waved back and smiled. "Tom's here."

Evangeline glanced over her shoulder, and a polite smile crossed her lips. "Hey there, Tom. We've missed seeing you at Friday night dinners."

"I've missed you all as well."

Tom cut a handsome figure in an expensive-looking gray wool overcoat. His dark hair never looked out of place despite the wave running through it, and his beard was perfectly trimmed. He smiled at Evangeline and unbuttoned his coat, revealing a black suit beneath.

"Winter is often our busiest season at the funeral home, I'm afraid."

"That's what Charlie said. Hopefully, things will slow down for you soon. We'd love to see you." Evangeline reached over and gave one of Charlie's hands a squeeze. "We'll talk more soon?"

"Of course." The smile that stretched Charlie's lips felt thin and weak. Fake. The flutter of panic in her chest at the thought of her aunt's disappointment with her didn't help. Charlie wasn't the only one in the family with strong intuition. What if Evangeline had guessed that Charlie was no longer the witch everyone thought she was?

Evangeline rose from her chair so Tom could take her seat. Tom grabbed her coat from the back of the chair and held it up. Evangeline slipped her arms inside then buttoned it up with deft fingers.

"I'll be so glad when spring gets here," Evangeline said. She wrapped her scarf around her neck. "I swear this has been the coldest winter I can remember, and I can remember pretty far back."

"It is unusual," Tom agreed. He slipped out of his coat and folded it over the back of the chair next to his before he took a seat across from Charlie.

"Y'all have a nice dinner." Evangeline waved and walked away. The bell over the door jangled Charlie's nerves, and she picked up the menu and began to peruse it.

Tom caught the waitress's attention and the short stout woman with the round, lined face approached the table with a smile.

"Y'all ready to order?" She pulled a pen from behind her ear and perched the tip against the pad in her hand.

"I've only just arrived, so I haven't had time to look at the menu yet. Could I have a glass of iced tea, please?" Tom oozed charm almost anytime he spoke, and it amused Charlie to watch the waitress's body respond, with a little step forward and an unconscious twitch of her lips into a vapid smile.

"Of course." The waitress practically giggled.

"Are there any specials tonight?" Tom asked.

"They're all laid out in the menu." The waitress pointed to a printout tucked inside the menu. "How 'bout you, hon? You want some iced tea, too?"

"No, thank you. Could I have some more coffee?" Charlie held up her now empty cup.

"Sure thing."

Tom laced his fingers together and rested his hands on the table. "So, how many cups is that today?"

Charlie reached for a couple of sugar packets and put them next to her cup, ignoring his question.

"Charlie?"

"Um..." She shrugged and met his steady gaze. "Maybe my fifth? I'm not really counting."

"You're not going to sleep well with that much caffeine in your system."

"I'll be fine. You can keep me entertained to pass the time." She reached across the table and touched his hand. A cold pang spread through her chest when he pulled away. He picked up the menu and opened it flat on the table. Charlie stared at the top of his head.

Tom had been one of the few people she could not read. So being unable to feel the emotions swirling through him was nothing new, but even without her gift, she could read his body language. The stiffness of his shoulders. The irritated intonation in his voice. The drumming of his pinky finger against the table as he pored over the menu.

Charlie was thankful when the waitress returned, carrying a glass of iced tea in one hand and the steaming coffee pot in the other. Charlie sat up straight and pushed her cup to the edge of the table.

"So, how're we doing over here?" the waitress asked. Charlie read the silver name tag with the name Gillian etched into it. Gillian filled Charlie's cup and placed the iced tea on the table next to Tom.

"I know what I want," Charlie said. "You ready, honey?"

"Mmm." Tom didn't look up. Charlie didn't take that as a good sign. She forced a smile and gave the waitress her full attention.

"I'll go first while he decides," Charlie said. "I want the pork chop special, please."

Gillian put the coffee pot on the table and retrieved her order pad from her apron. She took her pen from behind her ear again and scribbled down Charlie's order.

"Are green beans okay for your side, or do you want to substitute something else?"

"Green beans are fine. I'll take a biscuit instead of cornbread, though."

Gillian mouthed the word biscuit while writing it, then looked up, her gaze on Tom. "How 'bout you, hon?"

Tom sighed and glanced up. "I think I'll just have a cup of the white chicken chili please. And I'll take cornbread."

"You got it." Gillian tucked her pen behind her ear and walked away.

Tom took a sip of his tea and averted his eyes.

"Okay — did someone pee in your cornflakes this morning?" Charlie leaned forward and put her elbows on the table with her arms folded in front of her body.

"I don't even know what that means," Tom said, his voice as flat as his golden-brown eyes.

"It means you're acting pissed about something, but I'm not sure exactly what."

"I'm not pissed about anything," he muttered, emphasizing the word anything.

"You know we agreed a long time ago not to play head games."

"No one is playing a game, Charlie." The iciness in his voice sent a chill down her spine.

"Well something's going on. You're not looking at me. Your whole body is as stiff as a board. And that tone of voice you're using could stop the glaciers from melting."

"I'm not angry, Charlie," he said, his gaze finally meeting hers. "But I am a little disappointed."

"Disappointed?" Charlie winced as if he'd slapped her. Then her anger kicked in. "Pray tell! What have I done to disappoint *you*?"

"Did you think I wouldn't find out?" he said softly.

Charlie's stomach dropped like a frozen rock. Did he know? How could he? She hadn't told anyone. Hadn't even said the words out loud to herself.

"Find out what?"

"That you're not being honest with me," he said softly.

"About what exactly?" Her cheeks flooded with heat, and her heartbeat sped up. She tried to keep her voice low, but all the anger flowing through her body made it hard.

Tom glanced around as if he was scoping out who might be listening. Palmetto Point was still a small town, and plenty of gossips would relish hearing a couple fighting in public.

"You haven't been going to Friday night dinners either, even though you've told me you were."

"Are you kidding me?" Charlie snapped.

"No. I'm not. I know something is going on with you. And has been going on for the last couple of months. I don't know what it is, but even Jen and Lisa have noticed."

"They..." Charlie blinked hard. Were her cousins gossiping about her? The idea of one of the surrounding people sitting in the restaurant gossiping about her was more acceptable to her than her cousins talking behind her back. They were supposed to be on her side. Through good times and bad. Isn't that what family was all about?

"They talked to you about me?"

"Jen did most of the talking, but yes. They came to see me and asked if I knew why you'd been so distant lately. Why you hadn't made it to a Friday night dinner in the last month. I was shocked and a little embarrassed because they thought I might have answers to something I didn't really know was happening."

"I work in Charlotte. That's almost a four-hour commute on Friday afternoons."

"I know. I've had to feed your cat in your absence," Tom said flatly.

"Well I'm sorry if opening that can of cat food has been such a burden," Charlie snapped. "You don't have to do it anymore if it's that much of a problem."

"Charlie, that's not my point," Tom said.

"Y'all's food will be right out." Gillian seemed to pop out of nowhere, startling Charlie.

"Great. Is there any chance I can get mine to go? I'm a little tired tonight."

"Of course." Gillian's pleasant expression never faded. "Should I make yours to go too?"

"Yes, I suppose so." Tom's heavy gaze didn't leave Charlie's face.

Gillian glanced from Charlie to Tom and back again. Her feet shifted, and she took a step back. "I'll just go let the cook know."

"Great, thank you." Charlie gathered her coat from the back of her chair and started to get up.

"Hold on, please. We're not done talking." Tom sounded alarmed more than angry, which was probably a good sign. "You can't just run away any time it gets hard, Charlie."

"I'm not running away from anything," she said and pulled her hand out of his grasp. "But I am tired, and I don't really feel like continuing this argument tonight, so I think you should just go home."

Tom's lips thinned and disappeared into his beard. "As you wish."

Charlie rose from the table and pulled her wallet from her purse. She dug out a five-dollar bill and placed it on the table beneath her coffee cup, then slipped her wallet back in her oversized purse and slung the strap over her shoulder. "I'm just going to wait for my food at the counter."

"Charlie..." Tom reached for her again. The feel of his warm skin covered the back of her hand, and he squeezed. "This is...ridiculous. Can we please just talk? You know you can tell me anything."

"Not tonight." She pulled her hand away, grabbed her coat off the back of her chair and headed toward the counter. Behind her the bell rang, and when she glanced back at their table, Tom was gone.

"Great," she muttered. "Good job, Charlie." She took a seat at the counter near the register.

"Did your friend leave? His chili is almost ready." Gillian said.

"Just pack it up with mine, and I'll take it if that's okay," Charlie said.

"Sure thing." Gillian nodded and headed back out to the floor with a fresh pot of coffee in her hand.

CHAPTER 2

C harlie curled up on the couch and tucked her feet beneath her. Her kitten Poe jumped up on the old trunk she used for a coffee table and began to lick the gravy at the bottom of her empty take-out container.

"It is good gravy," Charlie said and moved to close the container. She held her index finger out, and the kitten sniffed it before rubbing up against her hand in earnest. Charlie coaxed the kitten onto her lap, and after a few moments, Poe curled up, happily kneading Charlie's leg.

Charlie grabbed the remote control and turned on the television. She surfed through the channels, looking for something that wouldn't take too much brainpower.

A knock on the door made her stop mid-click. Maybe

if she sat very still, whoever it was would just go away. Her heart hammered up to her throat while she waited. Another knock, this time more frantic.

"Charlie?" a familiar but unexpected voice said. "I know you're in there. I can hear the TV."

Charlie rolled her eyes and clicked off the television. She gently placed Poe on the couch. The cat hopped down and followed her to the door. Charlie unlocked and opened it to find her partner from work, Will Tucker.

"What are you doing here?" Charlie asked.

Will pulled the screen door open and pushed his way inside. "I need your help with something."

"Well, please. Come on in. It's not like it's almost ten o'clock or anything," she said, not holding back on the sarcasm.

Will looked at the large stainless steel watch on his wrist. "You're right. We better get a move on. We don't want to miss 'em."

"What on the goddess's green earth are you talking about?" Charlie closed the door and shivered from the draft of cold air that had followed Will into the room.

"There's a vamp nest about forty-five minutes east of here. You up for a bit of hunting?" Will wrapped his hands around the strap of the weathered leather messenger bag he always wore. His blue eyes sparkled with excitement, something she'd never really seen in the two months they'd worked together at the Defenders of Light.

"Are you...are you serious?" she said, her voice rising in disbelief. "I wasn't joking about it being late. And we have to be at work early tomorrow." Charlie crossed her arms.

"So maybe we blow off work," Will said. "Ben will understand. Especially if we wipe out a nest."

"You are crazy, Will Tucker. Nowhere in the Defenders of Light employee manual is vampire hunting an acceptable trade-off for policing an entire country of witches."

"They police other creatures, trust me on that."

Charlie folded her arms across her chest. "What makes you think I'd be any good to you?"

"I've seen how you wield that wand of yours. You're also fearless. It's one of the things I like best about you."

"Fearless. I am not..." She stopped. Maybe he was right about that. Since she almost died, the only thing that scared her these days was her cousins' nosy concern. Charlie gritted her teeth and shook her head. "What exactly do you want me to do?"

"Just be my back up. You know, eyes and ears. Oh, and you'll also want to carry this."

He opened the flap of his bag and pulled out a machete. He flipped it into the air and grabbed it nimbly by the blade, and then offered the worn leather-wrapped handle to her.

Charlie grabbed the knife and held it up. A little spark of energy flowed into her hand, lighting through her like an electric jolt. Nothing about the dark carbon steel blade should've felt good to her – but somehow it did.

She frowned. "What am I supposed to do with this?"

"It's more of a precaution than anything else. But if, you know, you somehow end up in a confrontation with a vamp, and I'm not there, go for the head."

"Not the heart? I thought you had to stab them through the heart with a stake?" Charlie said.

"Nah. That's a myth. In fact, most things you hear about them are myth," Will said. "You in or are you out?"

Charlie chewed on the inside of her bottom lip. "I swear to Freya, if you get me killed tonight, I will haunt you for the rest of your life."

"Yeah? You'll have to get in line." A wry grin played at the corners of his mouth, and he looked her over. "You may want to put on something a little heavier than your flannel jammies, though."

"Wait here." Charlie handed the machete back to him and went to her bedroom to change.

THE DRIVE TO GARNERSVILLE ON THE EAST SIDE OF Kingstree took longer than forty-five minutes, despite Will's heavy foot on the gas pedal. At least he didn't want to talk. Charlie had never relished a comfortable silence more. What concerned her most was how unafraid she felt. Her heart should've been pounding at the thought of facing down a creature as dangerous as a vampire. Facing down a whole nest? Should've scared her out of her gourd and left her hugging her knees to her chest and rocking like a baby.

But instead, her fingers thrummed against the wand in her hand, and she couldn't stop tapping her heel against the rubber car mat lining the floor of Will's '68 Mustang. Even though she could sort of picture how things might go, the idea of being attacked and having her throat ripped out seemed like an abstract concept. Nothing to fear. She'd already been dead once and had seen the other side. Even missed it a little bit. Was that sick? To miss being dead?

Maybe sick wasn't the right word, but deep inside her gut, she knew it wasn't normal. Wasn't acceptable. In fact, her aunt and cousins had told her over and over how grateful they were she was alive. They had even insinuated she should be grateful, too, because of Evan.

But some part of her wasn't grateful. Some part of her wished more than anything to be back on the beach in her afterlife. She tried to shake off the thought. If she ever told anyone about these feelings, they would have her back on the crazy ward of the Medical University Hospital so fast her head would spin.

"So, we're almost there." Will slackened the pressure on the gas pedal, and his '68 Mustang slowed down. "We should probably talk about how this is gonna go."

"Okay." Charlie touched the cold blade of the machete in her lap with the side of her hand. "Are they immune to magic?"

"Um...You know, I don't know." Will turned on the blinker and slowed down enough to make a right turn. "I don't think so."

"Good. Then we should be just fine." Charlie tightened the grip on her wand.

"You seem calmer than I expected," Will said, turning right onto a gravel road.

"I'll take that as a compliment," she countered. "So how will I know if I'm dealing with a vampire?"

"Oh, there's no mistaking them. They're ugly bastards really, and the razor-sharp teeth have almost a mirror shine to them. You know that stunning spell you used on that case last month with the illegal immortality potion maker?"

"Yeah," she said.

"I'm thinking that one might work."

"That's easy enough," Charlie said.

"Good." He pressed his foot against the brake pedal,

and the car came to a stop fifty yards from a large weathered wooden building with faded lettering. The only words Charlie could make out were Ton Gin.

"What is this place?" Charlie asked, and unbuckled her seat belt.

"It's an old cotton gin. This area is full of cotton fields. But for some reason, this place went out of business. I couldn't tell you when."

"It looks like it should be haunted." Charlie noticed the long dark windows running along the top of the building just beneath the roofline. In another time, she might have been able to see the faces of any ghosts hanging around the place. But those days were gone. A pang of sadness squeezed her heart.

"For all I know, it is. But that's your department and not what we're here for."

"Right." Charlie stared at the decaying building. How many vampires could be hiding in there? In her eagerness to avoid sleep, maybe she'd not thought this all the way through. "Hey, Will, wouldn't it have been better if we came here during the day when they're sleeping?"

"Vampires don't really sleep. At least not for more than a couple of hours. The whole nocturnal thing is another myth, although they do like to hunt at night. When I checked this place out earlier, most of them were congregating inside."

"Great."

"So just a couple of quick tips. It's best not to run. They're more likely to give chase. Kind of like a big cat. You know, a lion or tiger or something."

"Great," Charlie muttered. "I'll try my best not to become prey."

"Good. The second thing is if something happens to me, and you can't get to my keys, there's a spare in one of those magnetic boxes in the left wheel well."

"Will—" Charlie's stomach flip flopped.

"Don't worry. It's just a precaution." Will hopped out and walked to the back of the car. Charlie followed his lead. He inserted the key and lifted the trunk lid, revealing a stockpile of weapons, mostly shotguns, rifles, and knives, ranging from Katanas to buck knives.

He'd strung a work light inside of the lid, lighting up the trunk's interior. Each weapon rested in a protective foam holder that had been specially fitted to his trunk. Two dingy canisters of lighter fluid and a long-reach butane lighter caught her eye. She tried to imagine why he needed those. Were they going to grill out later? But she knew that probably wasn't the case.

"Let's hope you never get pulled over for speeding," Charlie said.

Will chuckled. "So far, it's never been a problem."

"Good." Charlie reached in and picked up a brown bottle of liquid from a wooden crate holding a dozen more bottles just like it. A wooden divider between the bottles protected them from clanging against each other and possibly breaking. A piece of green masking tape formed a stripe across the center of the bottle in her hands with the words Holy Water written with a marker in a neat script. "So, I guess this isn't a myth?"

"It definitely burns them," Will said. He pulled a small rosewood box from a stack of two other identical boxes and opened it. A small silver flask glinted at her. "You can have this. Fill it with the holy water and carry it with you everywhere. Once you start fighting vampires, it'll shock you how often you run into them."

"That's not really comforting." Charlie took the silver flask with a cross etched into the side of it. The metal felt cool in her hand. "You know this really isn't my religion. I'm not sure these things will work for me."

"They're pretty universal for killing vamps," Will said. "No faith required beyond knowing it will work."

"I don't mean to get all philosophical, but who's to say that vampires aren't a part of the grand scheme of nature? Most predators are necessary for keeping other species in check. You know, like wolves and deer."

"I don't think there's anything natural about the bloodsuckers." Will put the box aside and took the flask from Charlie's hands. He picked up one of the bottles marked holy water, opened both vessels, and began to fill the flasks. "And neither will you when they start coming after you." When the water overflowed onto his fingers, he closed the cap, and handed the flask to her. "Don't be afraid to use it. It can distract them enough for you to get away if you get in a bind."

"So, it doesn't kill them directly?" Charlie asked.

"Only if you manage to pour it down their throats. But that's a pretty big if."

Charlie spotted an open box of empty syringes with large needles attached. "What on earth are these for?" She picked one from the top and examined it.

Will frowned and plucked it out of her hand. "That's a last resort."

"What do you mean?"

"If a victim gets turned, and doesn't complete the transformation and feed, some of the sire's blood can reverse the transformation." Will tossed the syringe back into the box with the others.

"Wow, seriously? I thought being turned was pretty much a death sentence. Or un-death sentence as it were."

"Not always. I can't help the ones that kill and feed. That's what clinches the deal." Will put the half-empty brown bottle of holy water still in his hand back into the crate. He grabbed a second machete and closed the trunk. "Ready?"

A strange thrill went through Charlie. Why was she so excited about this? She should be terrified. But she didn't feel any trace of fear. Just exhilaration. She pushed the thought out of her head. Fear had no place going into a fight. She shoved the flask into her back pocket.

"Ready as I'll ever be." She gripped her wand in one hand and the machete he'd given her in the other and followed Will toward the dilapidated building.

CHAPTER 3

The stench of rot hit her in the back of the throat first, making her gag. She covered her nose and mouth with the crook of her elbow, but it didn't mask the odor completely or the droning sound of flies.

"What the hell is that smell?"

"Vampires aren't exactly the cleanest predators on the planet. They'll often keep a kill around to feast on the organs once they've drained the blood."

"Ew."

Will pulled a small flashlight from his front pocket and clicked the button on the tail. The sound echoed through the dark vastness of the building, and a wide circle of bluish light illuminated the space in front of them. Will shoved something toward her.

"Wrap this around your face. It'll help with the smell."

Charlie took the crinkled bandana and sniffed it. A strong pine-like scent emanated from the cloth, which smelled a hell of a lot better than the stink of death surrounding them.

She quickly tied it around her nose and the lower part of her face. "What's it soaked in?"

"Rosemary and Thyme essential oils mostly," he said.

Charlie breathed in the fresher scent of the oils on the bandana, grateful they masked as much of the death stink as they did. At least now she could concentrate on something other than breathing.

The hair on the back of her neck prickled, and Charlie held her wand up. She wiggled the tip and whispered, "Alight."

The end of the wand glowed bright white. From the corner of her eye, something moved in the shadows. Her heartbeat thudded in her ears, and she swiped her wand across the space to her side. A white trail of light crossed her vision and made her blink. Something moved again. At the silence and speed of it, her skin broke into goosebumps. It had been stupid to come here. Stupid and reckless. She had Evan to consider and Tom. What had she been thinking?

"Will?" Charlie said.

"I know," Will whispered. "Get ready to do that thing you do."

Charlie nodded and focused on the spell in her head.

With this light, I stun thee into stillness, where you can do no harm.

The light emitting from the tip of her wand changed from white to blue.

"Hello, vampire hunter," a raspy male voice said. "It's been a while."

Will shifted his light and the vampire's face lit up.

The translucent pallor of his skin made Charlie recoil. He could've been a ghost, but no spirit she'd ever seen had veins so dark they drew a map across the skin. Dark purple-red shadows fanned out beneath its sunken eyes. His cheekbones looked so sharp they might cut her if she dared to touch him.

Vampires on television and in movies always had an air of dangerous beauty. Of course they did. How else would viewers fall in love with them? The reality of these vicious, ugly creatures would be so terrifying that the idea of romance would fly out the window. The ghoulish creature stared through her with black unblinking eyes. She understood why Will hunted them. There was no ecosystem that would survive with vampires as the top predator.

"Charlie," Will whispered. "Now would be good."

Charlie took aim, repeating the spell in her head. A

flash of blue light flew from the tip of her wand. The vampire became nothing but a blur of motion, and the spell struck something standing behind him. A loud grunt and a thud resounded through the wide-open first floor where large trucks once carried the processed cotton away. A wicked laugh came from behind her. She turned as fast as she could and found herself staring directly into the eyes of the vampire.

"So, you are a witch," he said.

Will pressed his back against hers. "Charlie, don't look into his eyes."

She tried to look away, but something about him made it almost impossible. Her heartbeat pounded in her head. She saw his nostrils flare out as if he were breathing her in.

"You smell strange," the vampire said. "No fear," he whispered and leaned in closer.

Charlie held her wand up, aiming it at his face, and he retreated a few steps.

He made a grunting noise. "You on the other hand, vampire hunter, reek of fear. Do you know what all that adrenaline does to the blood?"

"Makes it sweet and tangy?" Will quipped.

"Hmm..." Charlie, finally able to blink, couldn't resist. "Like good barbecue."

The vampire threw his head back and guffawed.

"Oh, I like you, witch. I think I may keep you as a pet."

"No. I'm too feral for that." Charlie flicked her wrist up and shot off a burst of blue energy. It hit the vampire squarely in the chest. He stumbled backward a moment. His expression was no longer amused. A few garbled words escaped his mouth, and he fell into the darkness. A banshee-like screech resonated through the air, and the flurry of the death dealers began.

Charlie and Will moved like dancers through the onslaught of vampires charging at them. Bursts of blue energy emitted from the wand in multiple shots. The vampires she hit stopped short of attacking her and fell to the ground.

She dropped her machete and concentrated on holding her wand with both hands. The last vampire fell, and Will hacked its head off. Charlie turned in a circle with her wand up, ready to defend herself and Will. She let out a deep breath, and the light at the tip of her wand changed from blue to white again. She pointed her wand at the ceiling, and a single burst of white light shot upward and exploded like a firework display, illuminating the eleven headless bodies encircling them.

"Holy shit," Charlie whispered. "You killed them. You killed them all."

"We," Will corrected and shined his light down at the floor. He toed one of the nearby heads and flipped it, face up. "I count eleven."

"What?" Charlie faced him.

"There are only eleven here. When I surveilled this place, I counted twelve."

Charlie turned in a circle, casting her wand tip down to light up the floor. None of the pale, lifeless faces looked familiar. Their lips had all curled into snarls, revealing jagged, mirror-like teeth and long fangs.

"He's not here," she said.

"I know," Will said.

"I hit him in the chest," Charlie said.

"I know," Will said. "But he was their sire. That makes him stronger than all of them."

"So, he just got away?" Charlie tugged the bandana from her face and regretted it immediately. The stench of the corpses surrounding them choked her. She pressed the back of her hand against her mouth and covered her nostrils.

"Oh, sweet goddess, why do they stink so bad?"

"They're dead. Some of 'em have been dead for years, decades even. You'd stink too if you were dead that long."

"Can we just get out of here, please?"

"I need to clean up first. You can go wait in the car if you want." Will bent down and grabbed the closest body and began to drag it by the feet. "And be careful. He's still out there."

"What are you going to do?" Charlie said.

"Do you really want to know?"

Will dropped the body next to one of the other

vampire bodies. He grabbed another body and dragged it by the feet, hoisting it over the legs of the other two bodies.

"No, I guess not." Charlie stepped carefully through the maze of splayed legs and arms. Her stomach roiled at the stench of rot and blood. Once she got outside into the cool night air, she vomited into a clump of scrubby grass.

THE VAMPIRE HID IN THE SHADOWS OF THE TREE LINE. He watched the witch regurgitate and wipe her mouth with the handkerchief she'd worn around her face. Had she used it to hide her identity from him? Was she that stupid? He had her scent now and would be able to find her from over a mile away if he wanted.

Her movements outside his haven without the vampire hunter struck him as curious. She acted as if all danger had passed. He could have her now if he wanted. Drain her body of blood and leave her on the hood of the vampire hunter's car as a warning.

But something about her wouldn't let him kill her yet. The strange smell of her lingered in his nostrils. He pondered over it, trying to figure out why she hadn't smelled like her partner. Why hadn't she been afraid of him? There had been traces of fear but not enough to tempt him.

Did she not fear death? He'd never known a human — witch or not — that didn't harbor some anxiety about the finality of dying. Why was she so different?

The vampire hunter emerged from the building, and the acrid odor of wood smoke and burning flesh stung his sensitive nose. He slunk into the darkness of the woods.

They would all meet again. He would make sure of it.

CHAPTER 4

Charlie arrived home at nearly 3 a.m., shocked to see her body, hair, and clothes spattered with a black dried substance she could only guess was vampire blood. After her shower, she fell into bed and slept a short but dreamless sleep. She rose at 5 a.m. to drink her first cup of coffee for the day. One day this sleep deprivation would catch up with her, but not today.

At 9 a.m., she arrived at work freshly scrubbed and free of any traces of vampire from her skin and hair. She swiped her badge and climbed into the crowded elevator leading to the upper offices of the Defenders of Light. As the doors began to shut, a hand stopped them, causing them to retract again. Ben Sutton stepped onto the elevator, glanced at the panel of numbers, and took a place next to her.

"Charlie," he said.

"Ben," she answered. The doors shut, and the elevator shifted upward. Charlie swayed a little at the movement. The elevator car stopped on the second floor, and several people got out. Charlie shifted her position, standing along the right wall. Three more floors before she got to her office.

Ben moved next to her and cleared his throat.

"So, I heard you had an exciting night," he said softly.

"Really? Who told you that?" she asked cautiously.

"Will texted me to let me know he's going to be late and why," he said, with no trace of amusement in his voice.

Charlie's cheeks heated and her stomach knotted. "Did he?"

"Yep."

The car stopped again, and three more people got out. Charlie held onto the strap of her crossbody bag so hard it made her fingers ache. The car stopped again, this time on Charlie and Ben's floor. The two of them stepped off, and the doors closed behind them.

Charlie swallowed hard and touched Ben's elbow. He turned and faced her.

"Am I in trouble here?"

"As your boss, I have no say in what you do on your

own time unless you do something illegal. And by illegal, I mean violating witch laws."

"So, what we did wasn't illegal?"

"Nope. Otherwise, Will would be in big trouble."

"He's not a witch, though," Charlie said.

"No, but he deals with supernatural creatures, which is pretty much our purview."

"Right," Charlie muttered.

"Why don't we go into my office and talk some more about it."

"I've got a bunch of cases to file." Charlie jerked her thumb toward her office.

Ben frowned. "It can wait."

CHARLIE SETTLED INTO THE CHAIR IN FRONT OF BEN Sutton's new desk. After their old boss Lauren Coldwater was caught trying to steal an immortality spell from a reaper three months ago, Ben had taken over her duties as acting director of the Witches Investigations Unit. It meant he traveled less during the week and was able to spend more time in Palmetto Point with his girlfriend, Charlie's cousin Jen Holloway. It also meant he spent almost no time working cases directly, which Charlie had to admit, she missed. Ben's sharp mind and keen insights had always made working with him fun and always a bit of an adventure.

Ben leaned forward, folded his hands, and placed them on his desk. He steadied his sharp blue eyes on her. Charlie refused to squirm in her seat despite feeling like she'd just been called to the principal's office.

"Vampires, huh?" Ben said.

"Yeah." Charlie's leg began to shake against her will, and she shifted it, so her toe wouldn't tap the desk.

"First time?" Ben asked.

Charlie shrugged. "Yeah."

"How're you feeling?" Ben's baby-faced features softened.

"Fine, I guess."

"It's just the first time is always kind of traumatic," Ben said. "Are you okay?"

"Oh," Charlie said, unsure how to respond. "Well, I'm fine. I mean, I've heard about vampires my entire life but never really saw one till last night. They look different than I thought they would."

"Yep. Scarier. Less romantic," Ben said.

"Exactly." Charlie nodded.

"So, no bad dreams?"

"No. It took some scrubbing to get the blood out of my hair, but other that..." She shrugged. "It's all good."

"I see." Ben nodded. She could feel him studying her, trying to figure out why she hadn't melted into a blubbering pile of goo. Maybe she should've told him about the vomiting. Would that make her seem less suspicious? Less...broken? "You know what I can't figure out?"

"What?" Charlie leaned away from the desk as if his words might fire at her like a shotgun, tearing through her.

"How does someone like you — a mom who's usually level-headed and empathetic—end up in some stinking warehouse, fighting vampires?"

"Yeah, I can understand that question," Charlie muttered.

"Did you even consider Evan? What would happen to him if you died?"

"Of course I did," Charlie snapped. Her cheeks flamed with embarrassment, and she folded her arms across her chest. She didn't like to lie, and she had just lied not only to her friend but to her boss. "And believe it or not, he'd be fine."

"Fine. Really?" Ben shook his head. "I don't know what's going on with you. But..."

Charlie's hands curled into tight fists against her rib cage, and she braced herself against the painful little stings harsh words could bring. Braced herself against denigration for not meeting some job requirement she'd either forgotten about or didn't notice in the employee handbook.

"I want you to know that whatever it is, you don't have to go through it alone."

Charlie blinked hard, confused. She let out a strange little laugh. Ben's expression changed from sympathetic to disconcerted. Charlie straightened up a little in her chair.

"I'm sorry," she said. "I wasn't laughing at you. Really. I just...expected you to say something different, that's all."

"It's okay. I'm just worried about you. And I'm not the only one."

"I know," Charlie muttered. "I love my family, but they want to be all up in my business."

"Yeah, they do." Ben nodded. "And I can't blame them, because they see the same things I do."

"What do you see?"

"Since the beginning of the year, you've been anxious and quieter than normal. You've also been hyper-focused on your cases. Which I appreciate, but..."

"But what?" Charlie said in a small voice.

"I don't know. I can't quite put my finger on it. Which is why I want you to know you're part of the DOL family now, and we take care of our own. If you need to talk about anything... anything at all...I'm here. Okay?"

"I appreciate that," Charlie said.

"I mean it. You're valued here."

"Because of my psychic abilities?"

"Not just psychic abilities. You bring a unique

perspective to our team, and a skill set that actually makes closing our cases easier."

"Right." Charlie nodded. It was on the tip of her tongue to ask, "What if that skill set disappeared like vapor?"

Would he still want her on the team? Would she still be part of the 'DOL family'? She really couldn't afford to lose her job right now. Better not to say anything. She could fake it for now, and maybe in time, her abilities would return on their own.

Please goddess, let them return.

"Thank you." She gave him a perfunctory smile. "That means a lot."

"I'm not gonna tell you that you can't hunt vampires with Will. But I do ask you to be careful. Will's been doing this since he was literally a kid. I don't want anything bad to happen to you."

"I promise. I won't do anything stupid. Honestly, I probably won't go hunting with him again. I mean, do you know how he gets rid of them?"

"Oh yeah," Ben said. "Plus — they really stink."

"They do!" Charlie laughed and Ben joined in. After a few moments, their smiles faded and the awkwardness she felt with most people these days crept up between them.

"I better get back to work."

"Sure. I've got a new case for y'all, so as soon as Will gets in, I'll come and give y'all the details."

"Great. I look forward to it." Charlie rose from her seat and headed to the door. She paused a second and looked over her shoulder. "For what it's worth. I'm glad to have you on my side."

"I am definitely on your side, Charlie. No matter what."

Charlie nodded and left his office. She wanted more than anything to trust his words. To trust him. Ben was a good guy, after all. But something niggled at her. What if, because of his new job, he was in the same vulnerable position she was?

Ben had been practically raised by the DOL when he was orphaned. When he said the DOL was his family, he meant it literally. She knew how hard it was to go against family. If he made an exception for her and got fired because of it? It would mean losing more than just a job. It would mean losing his family. Losing his identity. And she wouldn't put him in that position.

CHAPTER 5

Charlie glanced at the clock again for the fourth time in thirty minutes. She scowled and continued to digitally file the last of her reports on the DOL servers.

The clock on the wall read 11:30 am when Will finally moseyed into their office. He still wore his mirrored sunglasses and still looked a little hungover. Had he gone home and drunk himself to sleep? The long, jagged scar that ran along his jawline carved a pale, thin line through the thick stubble on his face. He grunted when he took a seat at his desk and then laid his head down.

"Good morning to you, too," Charlie said, turning her stool so she could look at him. "You look horrible."

Will didn't look up. Instead, he raised one hand and flipped her the bird. Charlie stifled a laugh. "I see someone's in a good mood. What happened? You didn't sleep like a baby after last night?"

Will lifted his head. "And you did?"

"Actually, I did. For the hour and a half of sleep I managed to get."

"Well, good for you." Will sat up and stretched.

Carrying a folder against his chest and a look of serious determination on his face, Ben walked into their work area with purpose.

"Good to see you made it in alive, Will," Ben said. He put the folder down on Charlie's tidy desk.

"What's going on, boss?" Will slipped his glasses off, scrubbed his face, and straightened up.

"I've got a new case for y'all. There's some travel, though. Charlie, is that gonna be a problem?"

"Shouldn't be, as long as it doesn't go on longer than a week."

"This one could run a little long." Ben pulled a stool from one of the empty desks and took a seat at the end of Charlie's desk.

"Okay, I'll call Scott and see what we can work out."

"Great. Let me know if it's a problem so we can come up with a solution."

"Sure." Charlie nodded. "What's the case?"

Ben opened the folder and motioned for Will to join them.

"There's been a mysterious death in a small town near

41

Orlando. A young witch was found dead in her home by a neighbor. There were no marks on her. Just a faded rash around her lips."

Charlie picked up the file and found the driver's license photo for Ariel Martin. Tight, honey-blonde curls framed her long narrow face. Despite the lack of a smile on her lips, her amber-brown eyes glittered with excitement.

"A rash? Are we thinking it's poison?" Charlie asked.

"Possibly. We need to take control of the case from local law enforcement and their medical examiner."

"You got it," Charlie said. She shook her head. "Nineteen. So young."

"Yeah, I know." Ben said.

"So," Will said, leaning over to look at the file, "maybe I'm missing something, but why exactly is this our case? She's only been dead a week, right?" He pointed to the date on the file.

"She may have been murdered," Charlie said.

"Yeah, but a full tox-screen wouldn't have even come back yet," Will countered.

"Doesn't matter," Ben said. "She's a witch. That puts her squarely in our jurisdiction, which means we investigate it. It could be nothing."

"Or it could be something." Charlie touched her hand to the young woman's face and closed her eyes.

Come on. She took a breath through her nose and blew it slowly out through her mouth. *Come on, talk to me.*

"Are you getting anything?" Ben asked.

Charlie opened her eyes and shook her head. "Not yet. I'll keep trying, though."

"Great. Have you got a bag with you? Y'all might be there a few days."

Charlie nodded. "I do."

"Good. I'll check in with you before you leave." Ben stood up and left the office.

Will waited until Ben turned the corner before he knocked on the corner of her desk and grinned. "Road trip on somebody else's dime."

Charlie shook her head and smiled. "And are you ready for a road trip?"

"Are you kidding? I'm always ready for a road trip. I'm driving," Will said.

"Great. I don't know which is scarier. You driving or me having to call my ex." Charlie rolled her eyes.

"THIS IS DR. SCOTT CARVER, IF YOU'RE HAVING A MEDICAL emergency, please hang up and call 911."

Charlie let out a deep sigh and waited for Scott's voice mail message to stop.

"Scott, I need you to call me as soon as you get this. There's something important we need to discuss. So..."

Will drummed his fingers against his desk, and the sound jangled Charlie's nerves. She reached over and stilled his hand with hers.

"Just call me back, please." She pressed the red end call icon and put her phone down on her desk. Will pulled his hand from beneath hers.

"S'that bother you?" A grin spread across his lips.

"Don't test me," she warned. "The mood I'm in, I will hex you."

"Oooh. Scary witch." Will raised his hands in the air and wiggled his fingers.

"And don't you forget it." Charlie rose to her feet and grabbed the folder Ben had left with them. "I'm going to go talk to Athena about running a couple of searches, and then we'll get going. Okay?"

"Sure. I'll be right here." Will leaned over his desk again and rested his head in the crook of his elbow.

"Great," Charlie muttered and left him napping at his desk.

CHAPTER 6

Charlie walked down the hall to Athena Whitley's office with the folder held tightly in her hand. Maybe it was silly to put her faith into database searches, but it always served her old partner Deputy Jason Tate well. It could serve her, too, couldn't it? Not every situation called for magic.

The strong scent of lavender mixed with white fir and sage coated the back of Charlie's throat when she took a breath.

"The cleansing is strong today," Charlie said.

Athena's head bobbed up, her red curls bouncing. A wide smile stretched across her pink lips, and her green eyes looked over the top of her computer screen.

"Hi ya, Charlie," Athena said in her eternally chipper manner. "I was just thinking about you."

"You were?" Charlie asked.

"Yep." Athena pushed away from her desk and stood up. "Ben said he had a new case for you, and I figured you would come and see me first. Am I wrong?"

"Not wrong at all. But then again, you are a little psychic. And I think you're also learning my process." Charlie said.

Charlie pulled up a chair and set the folder on the corner of Athena's desk. Athena quickly stretched her back, bent over and touched her toes, and then did a couple of side stretches.

"I've been sitting since I got here this morning. I'm beginning to feel stiff," Athena said. "Do you mind if we stand?"

"Not at all," Charlie said. Athena pressed the button on the front of her desk and a hydraulic motor came to life, lifting the desktop to a more suitable height for standing and working.

"That's very nifty," Charlie said.

"You don't have a standing desk?" Athena said.

"I don't think we do. I mean, it's already a raised desk, but I don't think it goes down," Charlie said.

"Are you sure?" Athena asked.

"Pretty sure."

"Well, if you want to acquisition one, just let me know, and I'll put in an order for you," Athena said.

"Thanks. That would be great," Charlie said. "Could I get a chair like yours, too?"

"Of course," Athena said. Charlie admired the mesh back chair with adjustable arms and a cushy-looking seat. Athena cracked her knuckles and placed her hands on her keyboard, ready to type in Charlie's request.

"So, what are we searching for?" Athena asked.

"I need everything you can find on Ariel Martin." Charlie opened the folder and slid it across the desk. "Friends, family, education. Anything you can find would be great."

"You got it," Athena said. Her fingers flew over the keyboard, filling the small office with the sounds of clicking keys.

"I love that sound. It reminds me of an old typewriter my dad had," Charlie said.

Athena didn't seem to notice her rambling and continued to type. After a few minutes, her fingers stilled on the keyboard, and a deep line formed between her eyebrows.

"What is it?" Charlie drew up next to Athena so she could see the screen.

"There isn't a lot of information here, which is weird," Athena said.

"Why is that weird?"

"Well, because the DOL has a file on every witch that's ever been born."

"Okay. Still not following you."

"So, let me give you an example. Let's pull up your file." Athena quickly changed screens and typed in Charlie's name. Within seconds, an electronic file opened, and Charlie stared at the first page, a collage of various photos of her at different times in her life.

"What on earth is this?" she asked. "Where did y'all get all these pictures?"

"We have a bot that goes out and scours the internet and social media for photographs. These are probably on your Facebook page. Or, if you have a website or YouTube account. Or, it could've come from one of your relatives' social media." Athena pointed at the screen. "I'm assuming this wedding picture belongs to your husband."

"Ex-husband. And I don't ever remember putting our wedding pictures on social media. I don't know if Scott even has a social media account. This is downright scary."

"It's the information age." Athena shrugged. "You'd be shocked where we find information floating around."

"What else does the file say?" Charlie asked.

Athena quickly changed pages on the screen, and Charlie scanned the information. The file listed the usual statistics: her name and date of birth. But then it did a deep dive into her important milestones. The date of her marriage, and then the divorce. It listed Evan under offspring, which set her back in her chair. Then came her family, her job history, and her specific, special abilities.

Everything down to her blood type detailed on one page.

How could someone's life be reduced to one page of information? Charlie picked up Ariel's report from the file folder.

"Hers doesn't seem to have as much information as mine."

"Yeah," Athena said. "I noticed that. It's almost like someone deleted the information."

"Is that possible?" Charlie asked.

"Well, technically, it's not supposed to be. But it doesn't mean it can't happen. I mean, you're still dealing with people for the data entry, and we're fallible."

"So, you think somebody accidentally did this? She has no family listed. It's not like she sprang full-grown from the head of Zeus," Charlie said.

"Like I said, weird." Athena peered at the computer screen as if willing the missing data to appear.

"So, what do we do? Is there a way to find the missing information?

"Let me do some digging. And while I'm at it, Charlie, I'll run her name through the law enforcement databases outside of our system."

"You can do that?" Charlie asked.

"Yep. I have access to the FBI databases. If a state has a database available, then I can access those too. I'm more limited on the state databases, though, just because not every state is the same. Some states don't even talk to each other county to county much less on a national level," Athena said.

"Anything you can find out would be great. I kinda would like to have something before we head down there and just start asking questions," Charlie said.

"Nobody likes a wild goose chase. I'll do my best," Athena said. "I'll text you as soon as I have information."

"Wonderful." Charlie tucked the report back into the folder and closed it before heading back to her office.

CHAPTER 7

Charlie's phone buzzed in her pocket as she made her way back to her office. She glanced at the screen and sighed. Scott. Even in a text, her ex could sound disagreeable with just a few words.

What's going on?

I need to talk to you. On the phone.

A second later, her phone began to vibrate. She answered and held her phone to her ear.

"What's going on? I've got a lot to do," he snapped.

"I've got to do some traveling this week, and I'm not sure when I'll be back," Charlie said.

"This is for your job, I take it?" Scott said.

"Yes. So, I was wondering if maybe you can just keep Evan with you until I get back?"

"That would be in violation of our agreement," Scott said.

Charlie's head throbbed at the mention of Scott and his damn rules. She closed her eyes and tried to will away the sudden pain. She stopped in her tracks and gently rubbed her middle finger in a circle in the center of her forehead. Why couldn't he just be decent for once?

"Scott, that's bullshit," she said over the headache, "and you know it. We can make exceptions sometimes."

"Yes, but if I do this, what's going to stop you from pulling it every week?"

"That's not gonna happen," Charlie said.

"I don't think it's a good idea. If I start making exceptions, then—"

"Then what?"

"Then nothing. If you want to give custody back to me, we can discuss that. Otherwise, you and I need to stick to our agreement."

"Why does it have to be all or nothing with you, Scott? I'm flexible on extra weeks when you want to take him camping or on some trip." Charlie didn't hide her irritation.

"It is not all or nothing with me. He's your son, and I just want to make sure he sees his mother when he's supposed to."

"You know, there were plenty of times when Evan was

small that he didn't see you for days because you were working."

"It was a different time. I was in a different place in my career. Now I have much more control over when I get home at night. I thought when you took this job that you were only going to be traveling every other week, and it wasn't going to spill into your time with Evan."

"Well, sometimes, when you're investigating a death, it's not quite that simple."

"What?" Scott said. "What do you mean, investigating a death?"

"What do you think my job is, Scott? I told you I'm an investigator. I am basically part of the law enforcement agency for witches. Don't you remember?"

"I do not remember you saying anything about being in law enforcement."

"Sweet goddess, I explained all of this to you. You never listen."

"I just thought it was more like you were stopping witches from selling bad spells and potions, like the one my mother bought," Scott said.

"I do that, too, sometimes. And sometimes I have to figure out why a witch has died."

"Why can't regular law enforcement figure that out?"

"Because witches are our jurisdiction, and sometimes things that kill witches don't show up at first glance. Even curses and hexes can kill without leaving a mark."

"My God, Charlie. Are you ...? Is this job dangerous?"

"Not if you know what you're doing, it isn't." This is the conversation she had dreaded having with him. She'd hoped it would never even have to happen.

"I don't want you doing something dangerous," Scott said.

"I'm sorry, but it's not up to you," Charlie said.

"You don't bring this shit home with you, do you? Is Evan exposed to danger?"

"Evan is perfectly protected at my house. I do my absolute best not to bring anything home."

"Just make sure it stays that way."

"Fine. Will you let him stay with you next week or not?" Charlie asked.

Scott grew quiet.

"I'm seeing someone, and we have plans for next week, so..." Scott said in a low voice.

"That's just great." Anger flashed through Charlie, heating her face. Spittle flew from her lips as she spoke.

"I can't believe you sometimes, you know that? Trying to make me feel like a jerk for having to work. You know what? Forget it. I'll call my family. Just have him ready Sunday, and if I don't pick him up, either Evangeline or Jen will."

"Now, wait a minute." Scott's voice rose.

"I have to go," Charlie said. Charlie pressed the red

icon on her screen and hung up before Scott could get another word in.

"Everything okay?"

Charlie turned to find Ben standing behind her.

"Everything's fine," Charlie said and shoved her phone into her back pocket.

"Sounded like your ex-husband might not be very happy with the situation."

"He'll get over it," Charlie said. "I just need to make some arrangements with my aunt. That's all. I figured this day would come at some point. And it finally has."

"I'm sure either Jen or Evangeline will be happy to help," Ben said.

"They will."

Ben stepped a little closer and lowered his voice. "You know you can tell me if you're not happy here. If this isn't working out."

"Ben, no offense, but this has to work out." Charlie met his gaze. Her heart thudded against her ribcage, and she tried to keep her panic from showing in her voice. "My old call center job has been outsourced, and to be honest, I'm not really interested in running a ride-share business just to make ends meet. I knew it was always going to be a challenge with Evan. I'll make it work."

Ben nodded. "Okay."

"Okay." Charlie nodded and let out a fluttery breath.

"I had Athena run a preliminary search for me to see where we stand."

"Great. What'd you find out?"

Charlie quickly filled him in on the searches and what they had found. "Once we get to Florida, I'll check in with the police. I'll get access to her house and question her neighbors. Hopefully, someone will know something and be willing to talk about it."

"Good. There's also a pretty centralized coven down there that splits into smaller groups. Find the High Priestess first and go from there."

"That's good information. Thank you. I may call you back for names."

"No worries. I'm here to support you."

"Thank you. I really appreciate that."

"Okay, I'll let you get to it."

CHAPTER 8

Charlie kept Ariel Martin's file on her lap as they drove south. Every hour or so, she opened it, placed her hand on the single page report, closed her eyes and took long deep breaths. She tried to force some sort of feeling or flash of what happened to this girl. Each time she opened her eyes, though, feelings of failure threatened to overwhelm her. What good was she to anyone if she couldn't 'see' beyond the normal anymore?

Charlie's phone buzzed in the front pocket of her backpack, and she closed the folder. She quickly dug her cell out, happy to see Athena's name on the screen.

"Hey Athena. You got something for me?"

"Yep. I'm sending something to your tablet. I found her parents, and I also found the High Priestess for the area. I gave her a quick call to let her know that two investigators would be in her area and asked her to cooperate fully."

"That's fantastic. Thank you. This will save us so much time," Charlie said.

"I hope so. I talked to Ariel's mom, and she was so distraught she couldn't stay on the phone."

"That is totally understandable. I don't know what I would do if something happened to my son," Charlie said.

"I figured if anybody would be able to relate, it would be you. Just don't let Will talk."

"Why is that?" Charlie asked.

"Come on, you know why," Athena said with a half-teasing tone. "He's so brusque."

Charlie gave Will a sideways glance. "Don't worry. I'll take care of everything."

"Great," Athena said. "You know, I really like being involved in your cases. I wish more of the investigators used all the tools we have."

"You know, one day I'm going to get you out on the road with us," Charlie said.

"Cool. I would love that," Athena said, and the call ended.

"Fresh leads, I take it?" Will said.

"I've got addresses for her family and for the High Priestess in the area. Once we get settled at the hotel, I'll give them a call and see if they're available for questioning in the morning," Charlie said.

"Sounds good," Will said. A sly grin crossed his face. "And she's not wrong, you know. I am brusque."

"So, you were eavesdropping?" Charlie said.

"You hang around vampires long enough, you learn how to hear like them," he said.

Charlie's phone rang in her hand. A picture of her old partner Jason Tate popped up and sent a fresh wave of dread through her. His calls had declined over the last couple of months, but when he did call, it was to ask for her help with a case. So far, she'd been able to avoid him pelting her with questions she could no longer answer. She contemplated ignoring the call so he could leave a message.

"You gonna get that?"

She shrugged. The problem with putting Jason off again was it might cause more alarm to spread through the family. Her aunt already wanted to catch up. If she didn't answer, Jason might just say something to her cousin Lisa. If there was ever a case for not mixing work and family — this was it. Jason had firmly wormed his way into the family by dating Lisa for the past year. Lisa could wield words like a blunt object. The last thing Charlie wanted was her cousin's brand of concern coming her way. Evangeline's was enough. She answered.

"Hello," Charlie said.

"Hey. Long time no talk," Jason said. He sounded excited.

"Yeah, I know."

"I was beginning to think you might be avoiding me. But I couldn't think of what I'd done to piss you off."

"I'm not pissed at you, Jason. I've just been really busy. That's all. How are you doing?" Charlie asked.

"I'm doing okay," Jason said. "Is there any chance I could get you to pop by the station today and maybe help me out on a case?"

"I'm sorry. I'm on my way to Florida."

"You going to Disney World?"

"No, nothing like that. I'm going to investigate the death of a young witch."

"A case, huh?"

"Yeah, she died under mysterious circumstances, so we're going to check it out."

"Murder?"

"Not sure yet."

"You have the details?"

"A few. You thinking about helping *me* out, detective?"

"Maybe. You've helped me enough. Plus, maybe when you get back you can look at my file."

A fresh, cold wave of dread washed through her. The last thing she needed was to make a promise she couldn't keep. "It might be several days."

"It's okay. I can still work it the old-fashioned way until you get a minute."

"Fine. I'll take a look. But I don't want you to get your hopes up."

"No worries. Okay? I know you're busy. So, what's your case?"

Charlie opened the file. "Not much. I have a female witch, nineteen years old who seems to have died two weeks ago from unknown causes."

"Has it been ruled suspicious by the authorities?"

"Yes. She had a rash around her mouth, which was the only marking they found, but they're handing it off to us."

"So, what are you thinking? Poison?"

"Maybe. I'm hoping I'll be able to get some blood samples from the ME and send them off to one of our labs. We test for different types of toxins," Charlie said.

"Really? You have your own labs?"

"Yep, and our lab's a lot faster. I'll have results in a few days if I can get a blood sample."

"That's impressive."

"Yeah, I just hope the ME's cooperative."

"Just be polite and don't take no for an answer. So, your first murder. That's a big deal."

"I've worked plenty of murders with you and Ben."

"You know where to start, right?"

"Yep. I'm going to head to the police station first, then

meet with the family. I want to look at her home and hopefully get a list of her friends. Then I'm going to talk to the coven leader. See if there's any grudges in the community or anything like that."

"Sounds like you've got a handle on it then," Jason said. "Just trust your gut and remember that evidence doesn't usually lie. Can your lab test for DNA?"

"I think so." Charlie said.

"Well, good luck. If you need anything..." There was something nostalgic in his voice.

"I will call you." Charlie smiled. "And for what it's worth, I miss working with you, too."

"I didn't say that," Jason said.

"You didn't really have to," Charlie said.

"Get out of my head, psychic," Jason teased.

Charlie laughed. "I'm not in your head. Doesn't work that way. Especially not over the phone. I just know you. And your voice."

"Right," Jason said, and she could almost see him roll his eyes. "Whatever."

"Tell Lisa I said hey," Charlie said.

"I will. You be careful out there. Okay? Especially if it turns out to be some witch with a vendetta or something."

"I will."

The phone clicked, and Jason was gone.

"So does that reaper of yours know you talk to other guys like that?" Will said.

"Like what? Jason was my partner for a long time. That's all."

"Right," Will said.

"Hey! Just because we were partners doesn't mean anything untoward was going on. He happens to be dating my cousin."

"Fine. We're almost there." Will pulled into the farthest right lane and took the next exit. Charlie couldn't wait to get settled in a hotel room, get in a hot shower, have some food delivered and spend some time apart from Will for at least eight hours.

"You want to grab some dinner with me?" he asked as he pulled into the Holiday Inn Express.

"No, I just want to relax and get some sleep. You should do the same. You look like hell."

"Yeah, I'll get right on that," he said, but his sarcastic tone told Charlie that he had no plans of going to his room and getting a good night sleep. If he wanted to hunt vampires in a strange city, she wouldn't stop him, but she certainly wasn't joining in either. She'd had her fill of vampires and would be perfectly happy if she never saw another one as long as she lived.

CHAPTER 9

The vampire adjusted his glasses, pushing them up high on his long, thin nose. His frameless lenses were tinted blue and colored a deep gray in bright sun. They offered no correction to his extraordinary vision, but they did protect his sensitive eyes in both sunlight and the harsh manufactured light of the humans. Contrary to the myths about his kind that movies and television seemed to perpetuate, he wouldn't burst into flames if the sunlight touched his bare skin. Most of the myths were funny to him, but one left a bad taste in his mouth.

No matter what the world thought, vampires were not truly immortal. Oh, yes, they could live for many centuries, but it didn't mean the sharp side of a blade couldn't remove his head from his body. And while some of his kind were stupid enough to think themselves truly incapable of death, he was not one of them. He knew his limitations. And right now, he also knew that he would not give the vampire hunter and witch who had taken out his whole family the chance to kill him, too.

He hunkered down in the front seat of the black BMW in the parking lot of the hotel where the two vampire murderers had checked in a few hours ago. He loved a fast, luxurious car, and the sleek little sedan had fit the bill, so he'd liberated it for this journey.

Once the vampire hunter had disappeared inside the hotel, the vampire played a game of possibilities. He knew this hunter well. Knew that Will Tucker could not sit still. He would leave his hotel as soon as it was dark enough and search out the first nest he could find. The real question was whether the witch would go with him, too. Or would she let him go alone? From her strong reaction to the death of the vampire's progeny, he guessed the vampire hunter would be on his own. And that suited him just fine.

As soon as he tracked the vampire hunter's direction, he would find the local sire and make himself known. Vampires, much like feral cats, maintained a territory and kept themselves in colonies. A nest might have ten to twenty vampires, and as many as ten nests in a colony. Whether the sire in this area ruled a nest or the whole colony, the vampire didn't know. Regardless, he would warn the sire about the vampire hunter and would offer to stand with the sire to protect his progeny.

Once they had defeated the vampire hunter, the witch would be vulnerable. The thought made his mouth salivate.

The vampire hunter emerged from the hotel just as he predicted—alone. An interesting turn but not completely unexpected. A strange energy had passed between the witch and the vampire hunter when he'd watched them burn his home to the ground last night. They were not friends. Nor were they lovers. He barely remembered being human almost five hundred years ago, and things had changed tremendously in that time, especially between men and women. But he sensed a greater tension between them. And it made him wonder why they had traveled so far from home. And why was the witch with him? Surely, it wasn't just for vampire hunting.

The vampire hunter climbed into his car and started the engine. Once the hunter's Mustang pulled out of the parking lot, the vampire put the BMW in gear and followed the vampire hunter into the perfect gray light of twilight. He loved a game of cat and mouse.

CHARLIE SAT AT THE LITTLE DESK IN HER HOTEL ROOM WITH a notepad in front of her. She wrote down questions to ask the girl's parents. How weird would it be if she brought notes with her? She wanted to sound natural, but since she could no longer sense thoughts, preparation seemed like a better idea than just winging it. The last thing she aimed to do was to cause the Martins more pain.

A loud knock on the door broke her reverie. She glanced down at her watch. It read 10:35 p.m. She made sure to check the peephole in the door before opening. Will stood outside, shifting from foot to foot like a lizard on hot sand. Charlie unbolted the locks and opened the door.

"You're in your pajamas," he said.

"Yeah, that happens when I get ready for bed."

"How quick can you get dressed?"

"Will, I know what you're gonna say, and the answer is no. We spent nearly seven hours in a car today, and we've got a big day tomorrow."

"I know, but I found a nest. It's pretty active. I think if we hit it tonight, we can wipe it out quickly.

"No." Charlie crossed her arms. "It's late. I'm tired, and we're meeting with her mother at nine in the morning. Plus, vampire hunting is not our main objective."

"It's only a small nest."

"I don't care. I'm a witch. You work as an investigator for a witch's organization. What part of that don't you understand?"

"I understand perfectly, but when you find a nest, you have to act quick, otherwise they could clear out."

"So, let them clear out. Aren't there other vampire hunters out there?"

"Of course, but—"

"No buts. Why don't you go to your room and get some sleep? You did most of the driving today. Aren't you tired?"

"Not really. I'm all amped up, and I don't need that much sleep."

"Well, I do. You know I can give you something that'll help you relax."

"Yeah, that's all I need is to be unable to wake up because of some witch's brew. No, thanks." He waved her off.

"So, it's bad dreams," she said.

"Just stay out of my head, witch," he snapped.

"I don't have to be inside your head to understand bad dreams. I've had them my whole life, and I have things with me that will help. Please. Let me help you."

"If you really want to help me, then put some clothes on and let's go clean out this nest."

Charlie scowled and shook her head. "No. I'm sorry, but this is not why I came here. I need some sleep, and from the bags under your eyes, you do, too. Come on, let me help. Really, all it will take is a very quick spell and a couple of powerful crystals."

"No. Just — forget it." He huffed and waved his hands in the air before he quickly walked away. Charlie followed him into the hallway but kept her hand pressed against the door so it wouldn't close behind her and lock her out.

"Come on, Will. Don't go away mad," she called.

Will stopped halfway down the corridor, turned around and stalked back toward her.

"I thought you were going to be my partner."

"I am your partner, but not when it comes to ..." She gritted her teeth together and glanced down the empty hallway. "Listen, we're here for one reason, and it's not to go freaking vampire hunting." She mouthed the last two words. "That's not what I get paid to do."

"Yeah, you're right. It's not. And I guess that's what it's all about for you, isn't it? Your paycheck."

"Screw you. I'm going to do the job Ben sent me to do. And if you know what's best for you, you'll join me."

"You threatening me?"

"No, but I'm not lying for you either. If Ben asks me a direct question, I will answer him."

"Fine. You do what you have to do. I'm gonna go clean this nest."

"Fine. Go!" She met his icy gaze with her own angry stare. When he turned and walked away, part of her wanted to yell after him to come back and at least tell her where he was going. Just in case.

"Dammit," she muttered under her breath and went back inside her room. She plopped down on the bed and picked up her phone. Should she call him, or should she call Ben? This really had to stop. Will was going to get himself killed. Her thumb hovered over his name in her contacts list. She finally touched it and selected Message.

At least tell me where you're going, please. She waited for the three dots to appear on the screen to show he'd at least read the text. But the screen remained dark. She put the phone aside and grabbed her notes off the small table. A moment later, the phone buzzed on her bed, startling her.

1215 Harcourt Street. In case you change your mind.

I won't, but thank you. Just be careful, okay?

I am always careful. It's my middle name.

Of course it was. She couldn't help the grin tugging at her lips.

See you in the morning?

Yep. See you then.

Charlie closed the app, unable to shake the sick feeling in her stomach. She was going to have to tell Ben that Will's insistence on vampire hunting was out of control.

"Not tonight you don't," she said aloud and slid her phone onto the nightstand. She turned off the lights and crawled beneath the comforter. "Not tonight."

CHAPTER 10

Charlie stared at the ceiling, listening to the drone of the air conditioner. Some part of her listened for the sound of Will's door opening and closing, but it never came.

She pushed the comforter off, but that didn't help. Sweat clung to the back of her legs and her neck. After a few moments, she got up and checked the air conditioner.

Cold air blew over her fingers when she held her hand over the vent, but it didn't seem to be cooling the whole room. With a twist of a knob, she cranked up the fan, making the unit work even harder. She lifted the edge of her nightshirt and let the air blow against her skin, cooling off her hot body.

As she stood, lost in the refreshing jets of air, her

phone vibrated on the nightstand. She dropped her nightshirt and quickly made her way over to the bed, expecting to hear from Will.

But the name on the screen surprised her a little. It was Tom. The tired smile stretched her lips despite the 1:00 a.m. text.

Are you still awake?

Hi. I am.

I've been thinking about you. I didn't like the way we left things the other night.

Same here. I'm not in town, though.

Where are you?

Florida. I have a case.

Who's taking care of Poe?

Jen and Evangeline.

Can I see you? I'd rather do this face-to-face.

Do what?

We should talk.

Charlie's heart leaped into her throat. A sudden pang of fear threatened to choke her.

Talk about what?

How much I miss your face.

A little laugh of relief escaped Charlie's lips.

Oh, thank goddess. I thought you wanted to break up.

What? No!

I miss your face, too. If I call to you, will you hear me?

Yes. I will hear you wherever you are in the world.

A warmth filled Charlie's chest at that thought. Wherever she was in the world, Tom could hear her — all she had to do was call to him.

Charlie sat up in her bed and put the phone down on the nightstand. She closed her eyes. Pictured his handsome face.

"Tom Sharon, I want you," she whispered. A moment later a dark form began to stir at the end of the bed. The form swirled into a familiar shape as he appeared, and for a brief second, she saw him in his true form with his black robes wrestling around him and the stark white of his bony hands. She shivered no longer hot and when she blinked, his glamour covered his reaper form. Tom Sharon stood in front of her wearing a pair of black shorts and a blood-red polo shirt.

"Nice look," she said.

"You said Florida. I figured it would be hot." He grinned.

She crawled to the end of the bed, knelt in front of him, and wrapped her arms around his waist. He wrapped his arms around her, too, hugging her to him. The warmth of his body against hers and the weight of his arms comforted her.

"I'm so glad you came." She felt his hand move from her back to her hair.

"You are?" he asked.

"I am." She turned her head and kissed his chest.

Tom touched her chin, tipping her head up so she could look at him.

"Me, too."

He bent down and brushed his lips against hers.

"There, that's better," she whispered. A wide smile crossed her lips, and she wrapped her arms around his neck before she pulled him down onto the bed. He rolled onto his back, and in one quick movement, she straddled him. He laughed and rested his hands on her hips.

"Good to see you're still in top form," he said.

"You want me to move?" she teased and started to move off the bed.

"No." He pushed up on his elbows and dug his fingers gently into her thigh. She leaned over and kissed him in earnest. Her lips melted against his, and his fingers found the edge of her nightshirt. The warmth of his hand pushed underneath it, gliding over her back. His touch made her hungry for the feel of his skin against hers, and she peeled his shirt over his head, then cast her own shirt off and melted into his touch.

All the stupid, angry words they'd said to each other melted away like other people had said them a lifetime ago. She let herself sink into the sensations as her body joined with his, lost in the rhythm of their love.

CHARLIE DRIFTED, SNUGGLING AGAINST TOM'S NECK, breathing him in.

"So, your partner went to take on a nest of vampires alone?" he said.

"Yes," she said in a dreamy voice. "I hope he's okay."

"Does he do this often?" Tom asked.

"I'm not sure. He wanted me to go with him, but that's not why we're here."

"I'm glad you didn't go. Vampires are extremely dangerous," Tom said.

"That's funny," she said. "He said the same thing about you."

"Me?" Tom asked.

"You, as in reapers. He said they're more dangerous because they can't be killed, and they can be just as obsessive as vampires." She pushed herself up on her elbow and looked him in the eye. "Is he wrong?"

"I don't know about obsessive," Tom said, clearly not amused. "Reapers are dangerous in the sense that we are immortal, and we can easily take a human life."

"But you don't," Charlie said.

"No, we don't. We take an oath. It is our duty to protect human life. To protect the human soul and to transport it to its final resting place."

"I tried to tell him that, but he didn't believe me."

"I wonder why?"

"You'd have to ask him."

"I wonder if he had a bad encounter with a reaper."

"Maybe. Anything is possible."

He tucked her hair behind her ear and ran his thumb along her cheek. "You know, this feels good. Talking this way. I've missed this."

"Me, too," she said.

"Are you ever going to tell me what's been going on in that head of yours?" he asked.

Charlie leaned forward and brushed her lips across his. "I will. But not tonight. I have an early morning tomorrow. But after that, maybe we can get some dinner at one of the restaurants near the beach."

"I'd like that. Come on, lie back down, and I'll stay till you fall asleep."

Charlie nestled against him again and closed her eyes.

"You know I'm happy to take care of Poe while you're working."

"I appreciate that. Maybe you should talk to Jen. You guys can coordinate."

"I'll stop by the café tomorrow and talk to her about it." He ran his fingers through her hair. Her body felt heavy. Immovable.

"Good night, my love." His words flitted through her consciousness just before she slipped into a deep, dreamless sleep.

CHAPTER 11

Charlie stepped into the brightly lit hallway of her hotel and let the heavy door of her room close and lock behind her. She eyed the door next to hers and noted the Do Not Disturb sign in the key slot of the lock. The picture of Will snoring away popped into her head. May as well let him sleep it off. He must have come back late because she never heard a sound.

She hated to admit it but talking to the detective in charge of the case at the Sheriff's Department might be easier without Will. His scar, messy sandy blond hair, rumpled T-shirt, and jeans made him look less like a law enforcement agent and more like someone who should be sitting in the back of a police car. She'd donned a pair of black dress pants and a pale blue blouse with flutter sleeves and a sensible pair of leather loafers for her meeting with the detective in charge of Ariel Martin's case. She pulled her phone from her bag, copied the address to the Sheriff's station, and plugged it into her Uber App to finish the transaction. A few moments later, she waited outside for a white Buick to pick her up.

The Uber driver, Carl, arrived promptly and did most of the chatting on the short ride to the Sheriff's station. Charlie nodded and agreed when appropriate so she wouldn't seem rude, but her thoughts were solely on how the detective would receive her. Athena had said he was expecting her, but that didn't quell the fluttering in her belly.

When they arrived, she quickly tipped Carl on her app and went inside the flat, one-story white building. Her heart beat in her throat, and it was still too cool to blame her sweaty palms on the Florida heat. She'd never dealt with law enforcement on her own before other than Jason. Their relationship had been born more out of his doubt than her need to cooperate with him.

She pulled out the badge the DOL had issued and held the small black case in her hand. Should she just whip it out like she'd seen the cops and FBI do on television? Ben had never pulled out his badge that she'd ever seen. But he had a different approach in general. Working with the local Sheriff's Department made the most sense to her, and if they refused, she'd make do somehow. She had Athena on her team.

Charlie gave the leather badge holder a quick once over to make sure everything was in order. A gold metal, five-pointed star within a circle, glinted in the morning light. The words Defenders of Light were etched around the circle. The acronym DOL was stamped in the center of the star. On the back side of the star was the badge she wore to work every day with the DOL insignia, her name, photo, and title.

It all looked very official, and she held tight to it as she started up the steps to the main lobby.

Once inside, she found the reception desk behind a thick wall of plexiglass where a round-faced deputy with thinning red hair and a thick mustache stared at a computer screen. Charlie took a deep breath and stepped up to the window. She plastered on her most polite, professional smile.

"Hi. Charlie Payne. I'm here to see a Detective Blankenship." She held her badge up to the window.

The deputy glanced up at her from beneath thick reddish-brown eyebrows that reminded her of the Woolly Bear caterpillars that her grandmother, Bunny, swore could predict the weather.

"See that red band in the center of the caterpillar, Charlie girl? A wide band means a mild winter," Bunny had told her when she was eight. "If it's narrow it means a harsh winter is coming."

Charlie bit the inside of her cheek so she wouldn't laugh out loud at the memory.

"Do you have an appointment?" he asked.

"I do," she said. "At eight-thirty." She glanced at the wall clock hanging behind him. Five minutes early.

The deputy moved his fingers across the keyboard quickly, his mouth disappearing in a straight line beneath his thick mustache.

"All right. I'll let him know you're here. You can have a seat over there." He pointed to a small waiting area with a row of hard black plastic and metal chairs.

Charlie nodded and took a seat. She briefly contemplated a spell to make the deputy friendlier, but that would mean pulling out her wand. The last thing she wanted was to draw too much attention to herself, so she waited, but moved to a chair in the deputy's direct line of sight, so he couldn't forget about her.

Twenty minutes passed, and Charlie shifted for the third time. The backs of her legs felt numb and tingly. Finally, she couldn't take it anymore and stood up. The deputy didn't even glance up. She tipped her head to the right, stretching her neck, then to the left. Maybe a quick suggestibility spell might make him more helpful? She contemplated how she could do it without her wand but thought better of it. The deputy wasn't the real problem. He wasn't the one making her wait. That fell on the detective. She'd expected some push back. After all, she was from an agency he'd probably never even heard of, here to take a case from him. After working with Jason for almost two years, she'd learned a thing or two about how protective different agencies were over their cases. It meant he couldn't close it, couldn't get that credit, that win. Thankfully the DOL didn't operate that way. If she solved a case, it was hers no matter who else was involved. Her mind went over possible solutions while she paced back and forth. After another five minutes of waiting, Charlie wanted to get on with it and approached the reception desk again.

"Can you please see what's keeping Detective Blankenship?" Charlie said.

The deputy frowned, a look of confusion on his face. "I'm sorry about that. I didn't realize you were still here." He picked up the phone on the desk and punched in four numbers. "I'm sure he just got sidetracked with something."

"Sure. Thank you," Charlie said.

"No problem," he said. "Uh, yeah, there's a woman here..." He held his empty hand up and wiggled his fingers at her and hissed, "Badge."

Charlie scrambled to get the badge out of her purse again and slipped it through the opening at the bottom of the plexiglass window.

The deputy took the badge and turned it over. "Charlotte Payne. She's from the DOL, whatever that is."

Dread coiled through her stomach and tightened into a knot. Gatekeepers like this deputy could make things tricky. The detective may have been told about the DOL and why they were taking the case, but a deputy on desk duty wouldn't know who the agency was, and probably wouldn't care. She slipped her hand inside her purse and wrapped it around her wand. Maybe a spell wasn't a bad idea, after all.

"Uh-huh," the deputy said. "Sure." He hung up the phone and handed her badge back to her.

"Thank you," Charlie said and tucked the badge into the safety of her bag.

"I've never heard of the DOL. What do you folks do?" the deputy asked.

Charlie's cheeks heated. "Um... we regulate... um..." Where were the words when she needed them? She should've asked Ben about this. What should she say if they had questions like these? "Specific types of groups."

"What types of groups?"

"Um..."

"It's all right, Terry." A tall man built like a football player approached the desk. His cheeks and forehead shined with fresh sunburn, and he had an air of wholesomeness to him that reminded Charlie of boys from high school. "It's a bonafide agency. Part of the federal government, I guess."

"Something like that." Charlie smiled with relief at the man. "Detective Blankenship?"

"Yes, ma'am, I am. Sorry to make you wait. I had a phone call about another case come in that I had to take, and it went on longer than I expected."

"No problem," Charlie said.

"Ahem," the deputy said. "You'll need this." He pushed a plastic clip-on visitor's badge through the window.

"Thank you," she said and quickly clipped it to the collar of her blouse.

"Come on. Let's go back to my office," Blankenship said, and he guided her through the maze of the building's corridors to a pair of glass doors with Investigations in gold and black lettering printed on it. He pulled open one of the doors. "After you."

"Thank you," she said. She quickly surveyed the office. Six cubicles filled the space with tall walls on the ends and shorter walls between the desks, so the occupants could see each other and communicate freely if needed. A phone rang in one of the cubicles, and she heard another male voice answer it.

Blankenship led her to the last cubicle and pulled up one of the uncomfortable plastic, metal-framed chairs like the ones in the waiting area. She grimaced and took a seat.

"I don't want to take up too much of your time, so—"

"I thought there'd be two of you," he said, pulling his cushy-looking office chair out and making himself comfortable.

"Pardon?" Charlie asked.

"That lady I spoke to yesterday said you and your partner would be here to take over the case." He narrowed his muddy brown eyes. His face may have looked full of innocence, but his hard, resentful stare told her otherwise.

"Does it matter?" Charlie asked.

"Naw, I was just curious is all," he said, but Charlie got the feeling there was something else to it.

"Well, if you must know, my partner had a late night, so he's sleeping in."

"I see." The two of them locked eyes, and she refused to lose this little staring contest. She sure as hell wasn't going to let him intimidate her, regardless of his linebacker physique. Finally, he chuckled and looked away. "That's a tough break. Does he ditch you often?"

"No...not really. We've only been working together a short time so..."

"Yeah. I had a partner like that once."

"Hmmm." Charlie glanced around at the other desks she could see. "How many detectives are there here? Seems like a pretty big Sheriff's station."

"There's six of us. It sounds like a lot, but it's for the whole county."

"Right." She nodded and shifted in her chair. The backs of her legs started to tingle again. "You know I really appreciate you meeting with me to answer questions about this case."

"Yeah," he said. "No problem." He flicked the collar of his black polo with the Sheriff's insignia on the left breast. He wore his badge clipped on one side of his hips and the black holster with his weapon snapped inside on the other.

"I get the feeling that you're not really happy about this situation, and I totally understand," she said.

"Do you?" he said. A phone rang at one of the cubicles close by, and Charlie heard another detective answer.

Charlie scanned the room. "Is there someplace more private we could talk?"

"Of course," he said. He rose to his feet and smoothed out his khaki pants before he scooped up several file folders. "Follow me."

He led her down the hall away from the cubicles. She slowed when they passed two nicely appointed interview rooms that weren't currently being used and peeked in to see cameras in the corners and good-sized metal tables with welded rings to hold a cuffed prisoner.

Dan stopped at the door to a small conference room and ushered her into the room. A wooden table took up the center of the space and could easily accommodate eight people. A large whiteboard stretched the length of one wall, and beneath it a table topped with a stack of erasers, a large cup full of dry erase markers, and a roll of double-stick tape in a holder.

"This is a murder board," she said.

"Sometimes it is. Depends on what we're working on. We had a serial rapist hit the area a few years back."

"Right," Charlie said.

The detective took a seat at the end of the table and placed the files he'd brought in front of him.

Charlie walked over to the table and opened the top folder. Inside was the picture of Ariel Martin. Fresh-faced. Her dark waves softened her features and her eyes smiled, even though her lips didn't.

Charlie picked up the photo and took it over to the board. The tape roller squealed a little when she yanked a good-sized piece of the tacky plastic.

"What're you doing?" Detective Blankenship asked.

Charlie plucked a black marker from the cup and wrote Ariel's name beneath it. Then she turned to face him. "I think I know a way that will help us both out."

"Help us out with what?" he said.

"You're pissed that I'm taking over your case, right?"

"I didn't say that," he said.

"You didn't have to. It's all over your face and wrapped up in your body language."

He rolled his eyes. "It doesn't matter how I feel. The decision's been made. It's your jurisdiction."

"That's what the Sheriff told you?"

"Yeah."

"What else did he tell you?"

Blankenship folded his hands together and stared her straight in the face. The skin of his chest and neck turned red and blotchy as he spoke. "That you're a witch and that you work for some government agency that governs witches."

"And you don't believe in witches or magic or monsters?"

"Oh, I believe in monsters, but they're usually human."

"Yeah, I believe in those kinds of monsters too."

"My granny would say some woman calling herself a witch is courting the devil." He glared at her, his wariness rolling off him in waves.

"No disrespect to your granny, but there's no devil. Not like she means anyway." Charlie took a seat in the chair to his left.

"I don't believe in psychics and all that stuff," he sneered. "It's hogwash."

"I'm not here to convince you otherwise. I am here to figure out what happened to Ariel Martin. And I'm hoping that you will help me."

"I thought that's what I was doing." He pushed the files toward her.

Charlie touched the report at the top. "What do you

think happened to her?"

He looked confused. "What do you care what I think? You're taking this case over."

"If your Sheriff agrees, I'm thinking that it might be better if this case officially stays with you, and we work together. If Ariel was murdered, and it turns out to be some regular Joe Blow, then he's yours to take to the prosecutor."

"And if it's a witch, like you?"

"Then, I'll take the witch into custody and make sure he or she is punished."

"What about your partner?"

"I..." She fidgeted with the edge of the page in front of her. "I don't want to get into it, but I don't think I can count on him right now."

Blankenship's face softened for the first time since she'd met him. "That's a tough situation for anybody in law enforcement."

"Yeah. I'll handle it once I get back to my office, but for now, I'm pretty much on my own. You have a really nice facility here. Be good for interrogating, and I'd love to set up here and get your help with witnesses and documenting everything."

"We need to run this by my boss, but I'd like that. There's something suspicious about how she died, and her poor mama is just distraught. Ariel was her only child."

A cold pang pierced Charlie's heart, and she pressed her hand against her chest. "Do you have children?"

"I do. A son. Cole."

"I do, too, and I'd be absolutely devastated if something happened to him."

"Yeah," he whispered and stared at his fingers for a few seconds, his gold wedding band burnished against his tan fingers. "I'll help you. I'm sure my boss will be happy to accommodate you."

"That would be wonderful," Charlie said.

"My friends call me Dan, by the way."

"And mine call me Charlie. Shall we go talk to your boss?"

"Sure," Dan said and rose from his chair.

CHAPTER 12

Once the Sheriff agreed to Charlie's terms, she asked Dan to see the body. It took some finagling but an hour later Charlie stood outside the Medical Examiner's Office, observing the conversation between the detective and the young man seated at the desk. She looked casually at her phone to keep the guy from catching her spying. Charlie knew the ME was a woman. This must've been her assistant.

From his body language, the young man, his face too small beneath a mop of curly brown hair and thick, over-sized black-rimmed glasses, appeared unruffled by the detective's imposing size. Dan stood looming over him, but the young man just leaned back in his chair uncon-cerned and propped his ankle up on one knee. His blue scrubs pants pulled back slightly to reveal black socks and white tennis shoes.

From the looks of it, some serious back and forth was going on between the two. Finally, the ME's assistant looked beyond Dan to the window, and Charlie quickly glanced up at the ceiling, her cheeks burning because he'd caught her. It was times like these she missed her abilities most of all. Being able to get a read on what the ME's assistant was hung up about could come in handy right about now. She didn't dare look back.

Dan emerged from the office wearing a victorious grin. "He's gonna let us see her."

"Was that whole conversation about seeing Ariel?" Charlie asked.

"Nah. It was about the samples. He's not too keen on giving his samples away. He'd rather have our labs do the tests; in case it needs to go to court. Chain of evidence integrity."

"Right," Charlie mumbled. "Let me talk to him."

"All right, but I don't think he's gonna budge," Dan said.

"Leave him to me," Charlie said.

"All right, but keep in mind this isn't a big county, and some people get their nose out of joint over dumb things."

"I will do my best to remember that," Charlie said.

She gave him a grateful smile. "Thank you for talking to him. I really do appreciate it."

"You folks ready?"

Charlie glanced away and noticed the young man standing at the door.

"Hi," she said, approaching him with her best diplomatic smile. She stuck her hand out. "I'm Charlie Payne. I really appreciate you doing this."

"Yeah, well, Dan said you needed it, so…" He stared down at her hand with a familiar look on his face. How many times had she refused to take someone's hand? More than she could count. Now that she couldn't read another person from their touch, shaking hands didn't put her off anymore.

"We do. I know we all want the same thing." Charlie pulled her hand back and let it fall to her side.

"Sure. But for the record, our lab can test for anything your lab can."

"Of course," Charlie said. "If you'd like, I can get a list of things for your lab to test."

"But you still want the samples?" His dark brown eyes narrowed to slits behind his glasses.

"I do. But only for the same reason you do. To make my case in court. If we test it and find some poison you weren't aware of, you can still use it for your court case. Right, Dan?"

Dan furrowed his brow and nodded. "Right. That way, the defense can't pick it apart."

"Exactly," Charlie said.

"Fine," the ME's assistant said. "But you've gotta fill out the paperwork to have samples sent to your lab. So, everything's on the up and up."

"Absolutely," Charlie said.

"All right, come with me," the assistant said.

"What's your name, by the way?" Charlie asked.

"Steve," he said curtly.

"Nice to meet you, Steve," Charlie said.

"Uh-huh. Let's just get this done. I've got a long list of stuff to do before the ME gets back," he said, and gestured to the hallway behind them.

"Lead the way," Charlie said.

They followed him to a pair of doors with frosted glass windows and the words Autopsy Room painted on them. He pushed through one door, and once they were all inside, he let it go, and it closed slowly behind them.

The pale, sickly green walls reminded Charlie this was not a place of life but of death. A pristine stainless steel table with a sink built into it at one end took up most of the center of the small room. She tilted her head to note the fifteen-degree slant of the table, higher at one end and with raised edges all the way around. She grimaced at the reason for the table's design features and averted her gaze to the long wall with the three small metal doors built into it. Charlie had seen refrigerated drawers like this before in the ME's office in Charleston. Next to these units stood another metal door that reminded her of the walk-in freezer in Jen's café, except this one didn't store vegetables and meat. The black lettering on the door spelled it out clearly—Cold Storage.

Steve moved across the white and gray floor tiles and stopped by the middle drawer on the first row of refrigerators. He didn't wait for them to catch up and pulled the heavy-duty handle, opening the door. He reached inside and pulled out a long metal drawer with a thick, black body bag on top of it.

Charlie's heart thrummed against her rib cage. It had been a while since she'd dealt with a dead body. She glanced around, almost hoping to find Ariel's spirit lingering about, but she saw no sign of her.

"As soon as the ME signs off today, we're going to release the body to the family, so it's a good thing you came by this morning." Steve directed his comments to Dan.

"That's good. I'm sure her parents are ready to move forward with the funeral or whatever they're gonna do," Charlie said.

"Agreed," Dan said.

Steve unzipped the body bag and stretched it open so they could see inside. Despite the cold, the sickly-sweet smell of decay filled Charlie's senses. The girl's skin looked pale gray, and her lips had taken on a bluish tint. There was a slight blistering around the young woman's mouth, and the pattern reminded her of drool.

"Well, it could be Hemlock," Charlie muttered. "It can cause a rash when exposed to sunlight. I'd have to ask my aunt for sure though."

"Hemlock?" Steve said. "Is that even a possibility?"

"Everything's a possibility," Charlie said.

"I can't test for everything," Steve said.

"I know. But I think we're probably dealing with something herbal versus commonly known poisons," Charlie said and placed her hand on the young woman's forehead. She closed her eyes and took several slow breaths trying to clear her mind.

"What is she doing?" Steve said, his voice full of concern.

"I...uh..." Dan stammered. "It's just a thing she does. She's not hurting anything."

"No, she's not. It's just weird. That's all."

"Hush up, you two." Charlie opened her eyes. "I'm trying to concentrate."

Steve held his hands up in surrender. "Fine. I've got some paperwork to finish up. Y'all zip her up and make sure the drawer is closed when you're done."

"Sure thing," Dan said.

Charlie waited until Steve left the room and placed her hand across the girl's forehead again. She breathed in and out, clearing her mind, hoping for any sort of flash of what had happened. A face would be nice. A name. Anything the dead girl could show her.

Come on. Show me something, dammit.

Charlie gritted her teeth, trying to will something to happen. Anything related to the girl's death. But nothing came to her. After another minute, Charlie relaxed her face and opened her eyes. "Damn."

Dan stared at her curiously. "Should I ask?"

"You can ask, but there's nothing to tell." Charlie removed her hand from the girl's forehead, leaned over, and took a closer look at the rash around Ariel's mouth. She dug her phone out of her purse and took a couple of pictures and quickly sent them off to Athena in an email with the subject line: Can you search on this? Rash around the mouth? Causes.

"So, she obviously drank or ate something, and it caused this rash," Charlie said.

"Yep, I think that's the conclusion the ME came to."

"There are only a few things that could cause a rash like this. In the witch community, we use herbs for everything. Hemlock maybe. Possibly Belladonna. " Charlie clicked her teeth together.

"Would it taste bad?" Dan asked.

"Maybe. Some poisons are tasteless, but others are bitter." Charlie quickly thumbed through the contacts on her phone until she found her Aunt Evangeline's number. She pressed her name and the phone began to ring.

"I was just thinking about you," Evangeline's soothing, familiar voice said. "How's it going? You need me to pick up Evan on Sunday?"

"Yeah, probably. I don't see us wrapping this up tomorrow. It may be Monday or Tuesday."

"No problem, I'll go pick him up," Evangeline said and clucked her tongue. "I have a feeling that's not why you called."

"You are a very wise witch," Charlie said.

"What can I do for you?"

"How much do you know about herbs that can cause a rash — especially if ingested?"

"There are several that come to mind. How bad of a rash are we talking?"

"I'm going to text you a picture, and I'm sorry in advance."

"Why're you sorry?" Evangeline asked.

"Because it's of the victim. She's deceased."

"Oh," Evangeline said. Charlie could almost picture the scowl on her aunt's face. She quickly switched over to her messaging app and attached the best photo of the rash and pressed send.

"Okay, it's on its way to you."

There was a long silence while Evangeline opened the text and looked over the picture.

"Could be a nightshade, like Belladonna. Did she go to a hospital and die? Were there other symptoms that you know about besides the rash?"

"No, not that I'm aware of."

"Can you test the blood?"

"I'm working on that part," Charlie said.

"Good. Looks like that's the only way you'll know for sure."

"Let's say it was Belladonna or Jimsonweed or something like that, how could someone put it into...say their tea? Is it a tea leaf or an extract?" Charlie asked.

"Well, there are a lot of ways to extract the poison from the leaves or berries. Could be something as simple as crushing them and steeping them in hot water. Jimsonweed could go into a salad. It'd taste like any other leaf. Same with the leaves or berries from Belladonna. You could eat it and not know it until it was too late."

"What about the flavor?" Charlie asked.

"Oil and vinegar could mask it somewhat. Any dressing really if it was put in a salad. A tea might be trickier, but something strongly flavored like peppermint or ginger could hide it, especially if it's dosed with a lot of sugar."

"That's good feedback, thank you," Charlie said.

"See if you can try to find the source," Evangeline said. "Where would it grow?"

"Either one could grow in a backyard," Evangeline said.

"We're going to talk to her parents, and then if there's time today, we're going to check around the building."

"Good luck!"

"Thank you so much. I appreciate it."

"Anytime, sweetie," Evangeline said.

"I'll be in touch Sunday to see how it goes with Scott," Charlie said.

"I'm sure Scott will be just fine. Can you please text me his phone number and address so I can make the arrangements to pick up Evan?"

"Will do." They said their goodbyes, and Charlie put her phone back into her purse.

"That sounded like a very interesting conversation," Dan said.

"My aunt is a healer in our community, and she has a wealth of knowledge on plants." Charlie zipped up the body bag and pushed the drawer back into the refrigerator and shut it.

"Let's go fill out the paperwork. I want him to get the samples to my lab as soon as possible," Charlie said.

"You got it," Dan said.

CHAPTER 13

Juniper Martin's emotionless face didn't surprise Charlie. The petite woman, who had the same long, thin nose and full mouth as her daughter, curled herself into a blue denim chair, tucking her bare feet beneath her.

She seemed to try to connect to Charlie's questions, but as the conversation progressed, she stared off into space for a moment or two before answering.

Charlie wished more than anything she could tap into the woman's emotions and thoughts despite any pain it might cause her. Instead, Charlie had to rely on her other senses.

She moved to the edge of the sofa she occupied and leaned forward with her elbows on her knees.

"I know this is hard, Juniper," Charlie said.

Juniper nodded and then eyed the detective as he made his way around the room.

"Does he have to be here?" she whispered.

Charlie glanced over at Dan. He'd stopped in front of a picture of Ariel wearing a black cap and gown and the grin of a girl with the world stretched out before her. He didn't turn around, but the way he cocked his head told Charlie he was listening in.

"Would you feel more comfortable if it was just you and me?" Charlie said softly. Juniper's face melted into sorrow, and she nodded.

"Okay," Charlie said and touched the woman's elbow. "Hey, Dan, would you mind stepping outside for a few minutes?"

Dan turned his head and tucked his chin into his shoulder in a nod of approval. "Sure, no problem."

"Thanks," Charlie said. She waited until she heard the front door close and turned back to Juniper. "Ariel lived here, right?"

"She sometimes stayed with her boyfriend. But this was her home."

Charlie racked her brain, trying to remember if a boyfriend had been noted in the file that Dan had given her. It wasn't in the file Athena had compiled.

"What can you tell me about him?" Charlie asked.

"He's a nice boy. He and Ariel had applied to the DOL."

"Really?" Charlie said. "What position?"

"Ariel was gifted when it comes to plants. She could grow anything just about anywhere."

"And her boyfriend?"

"Chase wants to be a healer. He's fantastic with potions already."

"Is he? Wouldn't he be more use here in the local community, then?" Charlie said.

"Yeah, but they both had these big ideas. Believed they could help more people being part of an organization like the DOL," Juniper said.

"I see. Is Chase in your coven?"

"Oh, yeah. He and Ariel grew up together."

"Did you tell the police about Chase?"

"No. He would never do anything to hurt Ariel. He was head over heels in love with her."

"Of course, he wouldn't" Charlie smiled and mentally added, *sometimes we hurt the ones we love the most.* "But still, I'd really like to talk to him. Get his perspective on what happened with Ariel. Maybe he knows something and doesn't even realize he knows it. It's important that we speak to everyone who might have been close to her."

"And he won't be in trouble?"

"Of course not," Charlie said. *Unless he hurt her.* "Would you mind writing down his address and phone number for me?"

"Okay," Juniper said.

"Great."

"What about other people in your coven? Did Ariel have any disagreements with anyone?"

"No. Ariel was a sweet girl. Everybody loved her. The whole coven is devastated."

"I'm sure they are," Charlie said. "I'd really like to talk to your coven leader, too. See what she can tell me."

"Of course. Esperanza Guzman. Although, she's very busy. She's High Priestess for five covens up and down the coast, and she has her own business."

"I only need a few minutes of her time."

"Sure. I'll write her number down."

"Would it be okay if I took a peek at Ariel's room?"

"Sure." Juniper rose to her feet. "It's right down the hall. Last door on the left. I'll get you those numbers."

"Thank you," Charlie said. Juniper headed off to the kitchen, and Charlie went to find Ariel's room.

Charlie opened the door and was immediately assaulted with a cold chill wrapping around her like a mist. Charlie noted the vent in the floor and bent down to see if it was blowing, but no air, warm or cold, touched her skin.

"Here you go," Juniper said. Her sudden appearance made Charlie jump a little. "Sorry. I didn't mean to startle you."

"No worries." Charlie stood up. "Is it always this cold in here?"

Juniper folded her arms across her chest and rubbed one of her upper arms. "It didn't used to be. But ever since she passed away and we kept the door closed, this room just gets like this. As cold as an icebox sometimes."

"Thank you, by the way," Charlie said, taking the piece of paper Juniper held in her hand.

Juniper's gaze scanned the room, and she shivered. "Sometimes, I can feel her here."

Charlie kept silent, unsure of what to say. She could have agreed, and by the temperature of the room, she was pretty sure Ariel was still hanging around. But would that thought comfort Juniper or just add to her grief? She didn't want to risk it.

"Well, I'll leave you to it." Juniper hugged her arms tighter around herself and closed the door behind her.

Charlie surveyed the room, looking for any sign of Ariel's spirit. She also had her eyes peeled for anything that might tell her more about what had happened to her.

The tidy room looked like it belonged to an adult, not a child or a teenager. White walls gave the room a clean airy feel. A blue and white paisley comforter covered the bed, and a stack of pillows added to the coziness. A tall five-drawer chest stood against the opposite wall, and two matching nightstands flanked the antique oak bed. A tall mirror hung on the closet door, reflecting light from the two windows overlooking the back yard. A stack of books on one of the nightstands drew her attention, and she sat on the edge of the bed, close enough to read the spines of the books.

"You liked to read," Charlie said aloud to the room, certain that if Ariel was here, she could hear Charlie's words. The trick would be for Charlie to hear Ariel. "I like to read too."

Charlie picked up the top book and flipped through it. She frowned and put it down. Self-help books weren't really her thing, but from the other titles on the nightstand, they were Ariel's. Along with a couple of books on the history of witches.

"I'm sorry I can't see you. I used to be able to see and hear spirits, but I can't anymore. I know there must be a way for us to talk. I just haven't figured it out yet."

Charlie sighed, pondering her new reality. "If you can think of a way to communicate with me, that'd be great, 'cause I'm listening."

Charlie rose to her feet, and the bed squeaked. She looked inside the closet. Nothing stood out to her. Ariel's clothes, a mix of dress pants, jeans, and blouses hung inside, untouched since Ariel last wore them. They might remain that way unless Juniper Martin decided to give them away, which at this stage in her grief, Charlie didn't see happening anytime soon. She pulled a plastic shoebox from the top shelf and opened it to find receipts and several handwritten notes.

"Ariel, I'm going to take this with me, okay?" Charlie waited a beat and put the top on the box, closed the closet, and headed for the door.

The sound of frantic knocking on the door stopped Charlie in her tracks. Her stomach flip-flopped, and she approached the door with caution. She opened the door slowly and found no one on the other side.

"Ariel?" Charlie whispered and shut the door. She pressed her palm against the center. "Knock once if it's you."

One loud knock reverberated beneath her hand.

"That's good. Very good."

What are you trying to tell me?

"How about one knock for yes and no knock for no?"

Another loud knock.

"All right. Great. I've got a few questions," Charlie said. "First, did you know the person who killed you?"

Charlie held her breath, but no knock came.

"That's good information. Did you see the person who killed you?"

The knock started before Charlie could finish her sentence.

"Fantastic. Was it a man?"

Knock!

"Have you ever seen him before?"

Knock! Knock! Knock! Knock! Knock!

The frenetic sound made Charlie take a step back.

Her heart sped up with each knock and hammered against her ribs when the knocking jumped from the door to the adjacent wall. The picture frames trembled with each blow from the unseen hands. The sound traveled around the room then stopped abruptly. Charlie's breath sounded ragged in her ears. When the books on the nightstand flew at her, she didn't hesitate to leave the room, pulling the door shut tightly behind her.

"You okay?" Dan asked from the beginning of the short hallway. "You look like you've seen a ghost." He chuckled and approached her.

"I'm fine." Charlie straightened up.

"Whatcha got there?" He pointed to the shoebox in her hand.

"It's just a box of receipts and handwritten notes I found in the top of the closet. I thought it couldn't hurt to look through it."

"That's weird. I thought we got all the stuff like that when we went through her room the first time," he said.

"So...did you hear anything?" Charlie asked.

"Like what?"

"Knocking? Banging?"

"Nope. I didn't. Should I have?"

"Nah." Charlie shook her head. She pushed the box at him, and he took it from her without question. "I'll be right back. Then we can go."

"All right. You need help?"

"No, I've got this," Charlie said. She turned the knob and went back into the bedroom, closing the door behind her. The air no longer felt frigid, and the stillness permeating the room told Charlie that Ariel was gone. Charlie picked up the closest book to the door and read the title. The Witches of Salem, a historical account. The front cover depicted a woodblock image of people, mainly women hanging from gallows surrounded by men and women in the 17th century clothing that the Puritans wore. Charlie bent down and picked up the other books and stacked them neatly on the nightstand again.

"You used up all your energy," Charlie said softly to the room. "That happens when you get too excited."

The book on top of the stack flipped off the table on its own and landed at Charlie's feet. She picked it up.

"The Witches of Europe? I don't understand what you're trying to tell me. Do you want me to take this book?"

A loud banging knock in the center of the wall above the bed shook the framed mirror loose, and it crashed down behind the headboard. Charlie leaned forward to take a peek. Long cracks stretched from the center of the mirror, where it looked almost like someone had punched the reflective glass. "Great, now your mother's going to think I broke it."

She tucked the book under her arm and headed back into the hall to tell Dan she got what she came for, even if she didn't know exactly what she would learn from the book.

A chill settled over her shoulders, and she closed the door behind her again. A thrill went through her, and she had to fight the urge to grin. She could still communicate with the dead. Even if it was in a very limited way. She also knew that even under the best of circumstances, like when she could see them and hear them, spirits didn't always communicate in a straightforward way. That was okay. For the first time in months, she felt like her old self again. Maybe the dead still had a voice. She just needed to learn how to listen to it differently.

CHAPTER 14

Dan parked the unmarked Chevy Tahoe on the street in front of the house where Chase Andrews lived. Juniper Martin had given them the address. As Ariel's boyfriend, he was first on their list to interrogate about her death. Charlie scanned the property. The little bungalow matched all the others on the street in style and size, but the pale, yellow paint had come off in long thin strips in places. One of the white shutters flanking the two windows facing the street hung askew. Crabgrass and weeds had overtaken the once-green lawn in the front yard. In contrast, the other houses on the street, painted in ice cream-colored pastels, showed tidy landscaping in the front and along their side gardens.

"You sure this is the address?" Charlie asked.

"Yep." Dan tapped the screen of the tablet mounted to the center of his dashboard. "That's what you gave me."

Charlie stared at the darkened windows of Andrews's home. "It looks like nobody lives here." She climbed out of the truck and approached the picket fence. Someone had wired the gate shut with rusty barbed wire, and the outline of the missing sliding lock looked cleaner than the rest of the grimy pickets of the gate.

"Also looks like they don't want visitors." Dan pointed to the two signs on either side of the gate. One read *No Trespassing*. The other *Beware of the dog*. Charlie scanned the yard but saw no sign of a dog.

"Yeah, it does," Charlie said. She couldn't put her finger on it, but something about the house didn't feel right. "It is kind of strange how unkempt this place is compared to the neighbors. You think one of them would've called the county and complained."

"It's a possibility," Dan said. "I can check to see if there've been complaints. That barbed wire sends a pretty serious message. I've got some bolt cutters in the back of my truck."

"That won't be necessary." Charlie slipped her hand into her purse and furtively took out her wand.

Dan's eyes widened, and his eyebrows rose halfway up his forehead. "Is that what I think it is?"

"Yep." She nodded and touched the tip of her wand to one of the inhospitable barbs before she closed her eyes and cleared her mind. The spell formed with a little coaxing, and in her head, she chanted:

I call on the elements, earth, air, water, and fire.

Release the gate, unbind this wire.

When she'd repeated the spell in her mind for the third time, the heavy-duty staple nails holding the wire to the fencepost squeaked and wiggled before popping out and falling to the ground.

The wire hung loose for a moment before swinging away from the fence post like a plant tendril looking for something to grab onto. Slowly, it began to uncoil from the top to the bottom, until finally, it fell on the walkway inside the fence.

"Holy shit," Dan muttered. "This is real."

"Yep, it is." Charlie pushed against the gate, and it scraped against the ground.

"I didn't think –"

"I know. It's okay."

"Could anybody do that?"

"Um...yeah sure. If you committed to becoming a witch and learned to control your energy and intent. But it takes lots of practice. Kind of like shooting the center of a bull's-eye target takes practice."

Dan nodded. "Ah."

"Shall we?" Charlie reached on the inside of the gate and picked it up by one of the braces and pushed, opening it enough so they could pass through. Sandy soil mounded the edges of the decorative brick walkway in places, and Charlie could see fire ants milling about the hills. Maybe it was her training as a witch or maybe it was just her natural intuition, but even without her psychic abilities she sensed something off about the house and yard. For a split second she was grateful not to be completely blind to the fact that everything about this place screamed *Go Away!*

"Hmmmph."

"What?" Dan asked.

"I don't know. There's just something about the energy of this whole place..."

"Yeah. I know what you mean."

Charlie walked up the steps and noticed the screen in the outer door had a large diagonal slash. The hinge squealed in protest when she opened it. The dark red front door would've been pretty against the pale yellow of the house if the paint had not bubbled and peeled in places. There was no window in the door. Not even a peephole. She turned to make a remark to Dan but found him still at the bottom of the porch stairs with one foot perched on a step. His chest heaved and sweat soaked his shirt beneath his underarms and around his collar.

"You okay?" She asked. "You're awfully red."

"I...I don't know. It's weird. Like if I try to climb the steps, I can't breathe." He pressed his hand against his chest and took his foot off the step. He took a few deep breaths. Charlie joined him at the bottom.

"Tell me what you're feeling." Charlie pulled a clean bandana from her purse and handed it to him. Dan took it and mopped his forehead.

"I don't know. It's like...I just want to leave."

"Because you're scared?" Charlie asked.

"No. Not scared. Just like a bad feeling. I know that sounds crazy."

"It doesn't sound crazy at all. I think there's a spell on this place to drive people away."

"So you feel it, too?"

"Not exactly the way you do. I've got some protection in place that shields me from the worst of it. My badge, and also this." She pulled the silver pentacle pendant she always wore from inside her blouse and showed it to him. "This absorbs energy or reflects it away from me."

"Oh." He nodded, his mouth curving into a frown.

She patted him on his well-muscled arm. "Why don't you go back to the gate?"

"He could be dangerous. I should back you up."

"Once I get the spell broken on this place, and you no longer look like you're about to have a heatstroke, I will welcome you backing me up. But I don't want to risk you having a heart attack or something."

"Could that happen?" Dan took a few steps back.

"Yeah, it could."

"Okay. But you be careful, you hear? No unnecessary risks."

"Don't worry about me. I can handle it."

She waited for Dan to get safely behind the gate before she approached the door again. The sound of her knock against the wood door vibrated in her ears too loudly. She listened carefully for any sign that Chase Andrews was inside. The house was silent. Charlie stepped over to one of the windows next to the door. The glass was so dark she couldn't see inside.

"A concealment spell," she whispered. "Nice touch, Chase."

Charlie walked off the porch and halfway down the walkway. She gave Dan a reassuring wave before she turned and faced the house and extended her wand. The tip of her wand glowed blue with the energy of her concentration, and she waved it in small circles in the air. Round and round, the circles grew larger.

"I call on fire, water, earth, and air, break the spell hiding this place.

Fire, water, earth and air, peel back the glamour and reveal its face."

Charlie repeated the words until the edges of the illusion began to burn away. The last of the glamour around the house disappeared with a flash and pop that reminded Charlie of the Snaps fireworks she'd played with on the fourth of July when she was a kid.

With the spell broken, the bungalow shined, neat and tidy with freshly painted siding the color of lemon sherbet, bright white trim, and properly hung shutters. An unblemished dark purple door marked that a witch lived here. A bright green, freshly shorn lawn of St. Augustine grass emerged, and the weeds withdrew beneath it. Curved beds full of flowering perennials sprung from the scraggly brush in front of the porch, and two large birds of paradise dotted the corners of the house.

Dan approached her with his mouth agape. The redness in his cheeks had faded, and he breathed easier. "What the hell?"

Charlie smiled. "So, how are you feeling?"

"Better. Normal." He rubbed the back of his neck. "How—?"

"It was a glamour. An illusion basically, mixed with a repelling spell."

"So, all that was just to keep people away?" Dan gestured to the house and yard.

"Yep." Charlie nodded.

"Why?"

"I think we should ask him that," Charlie said.

The two of them marched up the steps, and Charlie knocked on the door again. She waited a beat. This time she heard movement inside the house. Silently, she signaled for Dan to look inside one of the windows overlooking the porch. Dan gave her a nod and peered inside.

"Chase Andrews, I know you're in there." She used her most serious mother voice. "This is the DOL. Open the door."

Charlie heard a muffled commotion inside, and a door slammed at the back of the house.

"Shit. We've got a runner." Dan took off toward the end of the porch. He jumped the railing with ease and disappeared around the corner of the house.

Charlie laughed and shook off the shock of his actions before she ran down the steps after him.

The houses on this street all backed up to a thick grove of pine trees, live oaks, and scrubby brush. Charlie relied on her long legs and sheer determination to catch up to Dan. In the distance, she saw a young man in a white shirt bouncing through the trees. A stitch bit into her side, and she stopped and pointed her wand. The tip glowed white, and she focused as much energy as she could muster into the spell.

Trees, brush, and vines throughout this place.

I beseech you now to stop this Chase.

She flicked her wrist, and a loud cracking noise reverberated like thunder across the woods. A large tree branch fell directly in the young man's path. He skidded to a stop and fell, disappearing from her view.

Charlie rubbed the stitch in her side until it was bearable and chased after Dan. A few minutes later, she caught up to him. He had rolled Chase over onto his stomach and had bound his hands together with hand-cuffs. Charlie bent over with her hands on her knees, gasping for air. If she was going to have to chase after suspects, she would have to start exercising more.

"How do I get him loose?" Dan pointed to the strong, thin woody vines wrapped around Chase's ankles.

"Sorry, my bad," she said between breaths. "I'm outta shape. I've got to get back to the gym." When she could stand up without pressure in her chest, she touched the tip of her wand to the vines, and they slowly recoiled.

Dan grabbed the young man by one arm and pulled him to his feet with ease.

"Come on. You've got some explaining to do. You almost gave me a heart attack with that spell of yours."

Charlie suppressed a grin. "Let's take him back to your station house to question him."

"Sure thing," Dan said.

"I haven't done anything." The young man tried to wiggle free of Dan's meaty hand. Dan held tight and pushed Chase forward through the woods back toward the house.

"You could've killed me!" Dan's small-town-nice-guy face morphed into chiseled angry lines.

"You don't understand," Chase said.

Charlie stopped in her tracks and touched Dan's arm. "Hang on. What don't we understand?"

"Why should I tell you anything?" Chase said.

"You know what? He's right. He hasn't done anything other than run from us. We should let him go. Although, good luck getting that glamour back up," Charlie said.

"You broke my spell? Who are you people?"

"I'm Charlie Payne. I'm with the Defenders of Light, and I'm investigating the death of your *girlfriend*, Ariel Martin." She unclipped her badge from her belt and held it up for Chase to get a good look.

All the color drained from Chase's face. "Wait. You're here about Ariel?"

"Yeah. But if you don't answer any questions, that's fine. We'll just let you go back to hiding in your house. That's what you're doing, isn't it? Hiding?"

"Yes. Are you really with the DOL?"

"I am," Charlie said.

"If you will protect me, I will tell you whatever you want to know."

"Protect you from what?" Charlie asked.

"From that witchfinder. He's the one who killed Ariel."

"Witchfinders haven't been a thing for nearly three hundred years." Charlie gave him a skeptical look. "And I don't know that they were ever a thing in this country."

"I have proof. Please." His voice cracked. "I just need your protection."

"Okay. You answer all my questions, and I'll make sure you're protected. But if I think for one second you're lying, I will bind up your magic so fast it will make your head spin."

"I won't lie," Chase said.

"Great. Let's head back to the Sheriff's station and talk."

"Thank you. Really. Thank you," Chase said. "Now, can you uncuff me? You know they can't really hold me for long anyway, right?"

Charlie touched the tip of her wand to the cuffs. "They'll hold you now. Come on. Let's get out of here. This place is giving me the creeps."

"Yes ma'am," Dan said and guided Chase forward through the woods.

CHAPTER 15

C harlie studied a large 24-inch monitor in the video control room while Dan brought Chase Andrews to an interrogation room. Once Chase had settled into a hard chair at the metal table, Dan read the young man his rights.

"Am I being arrested?" Chase asked, his worried eyes scanning the small, starkly furnished room. Chairs for two interrogators, and two cameras hanging from the corners of the ceiling focused on Chase accounted for the décor.

"No," Dan said, his voice giving nothing away as he pulled his chair up to the table and leaned forward on his elbows. "We just want to ask you some questions right now, that's all. But I read you your rights because you can choose not to talk to us."

"Should I get a lawyer?" Chase asked. Beads of sweat gathered on his forehead.

"That's up to you."

"Okay." Chase licked his lips. "I mean, I didn't do anything."

"Then it can't hurt to talk to us, can it?"

"No, I guess not," Chase said, leaning back a bit.

"So, you agree to waive your rights and talk to us?"

"Yeah, sure. Can you take these off me?" Chase held his shackled hands across the table and wiggled them back and forth.

"Sure. Can I get you anything? Water? Soda?" Dan uncuffed Chase and said, "We've got coffee and hot tea too."

"What kind of tea?" Chase rubbed his wrists. Charlie could only see the back of Dan's head and shoulders. His thick neck flexed at Chase's question.

"Um, I think it's Lipton. But I'd have to check."

Charlie suppressed a smile and grabbed her bag. It took a little digging, but she found the old mint tin she used to carry hot tea bags with her. Her aunt specialized in making herbal teas, blends of different tea leaves, herbs, flowers and fruit peels. Each blend had a specific purpose, ranging from boosting energy to inducing sleepy relaxation, from soothing stomach troubles to easing menstrual cramps.

"No, thanks." Chase scrubbed his hand through his hair.

"Suit yourself. I need to check on a couple of things. I'll be back in a few minutes." The metal legs of Dan's chair scraped across the cement floor when he rose to leave the interrogation room. He closed the door tightly behind him, and Chase folded his arms and rested them on the table. He looked around the tiny sparse room, his gaze flitting to the corners at the cameras trained on him. The screen in front of Charlie began to crackle.

"Well, shoot," she muttered. Electronics and witches often didn't mix well, especially when emotions were running high. She grabbed her phone and the mint tin, then set her bag down on the table next to the video technician.

"Where can I get a cup and hot water for tea?" she asked.

"There's a coffee station at the end of the hall near the cubicles."

"Great, thank you." She hopped to her feet and almost slammed into Dan in the hallway when she came out of the A/V room.

She grinned and said, "Whoa, who put a wall here?"

Dan chuckled. "He didn't want anything to drink. You want to let him stew for a bit?"

"No. I think I have something he'll want." She held up the mint tin.

"What is that?"

"Tea bags that my aunt makes."

"Anything illegal in there?" Dan teased.

"Not unless ginger, mint, and orange peel are illegal in this state."

"Hmm. Sounds like a weird mix."

"They're not all mixed together. But his anxiety is pretty high. Sometimes when witches get emotional, electronic things break."

"Seriously?" Dan asked.

"Yep. Last thing I want is for the cameras to fizzle out."

"All right." Dan nodded. "Do you want me in there as backup?"

"Why don't you watch for now? I'd like to see if I can get him to talk first. I want to know more about this…" Charlie glanced up and down the hallway to make sure no one else was within listening distance. She lowered her voice, "This witchfinder he was talking about."

"Right. You said they don't exist."

"Not anymore. Or least not that I'm aware of. I'm gonna give my boss a quick call and run it by him. See if he has any insight."

"Good idea," Dan said. "I'll keep an eye on him till you get back."

"Thanks." Charlie walked to the coffee station and filled one of the heavy paper cups with hot water. She grabbed a couple of packets of sugar and one of the half and half creamer cups in case he wanted milk in his tea and shoved them into the front pocket of her blazer. The hot water burned through the cup, and she put it down on the table so she could make a quick call to Ben.

Ben answered on the first ring. "Hey, Charlie, how's it going?"

"I'm about to go question the deceased's boyfriend."

"Does he look good for it?"

"Not sure," she said, leaning against the painted cement block wall of the sparse office. "It's a weird situation." Charlie described the glamour and how Chase had tried to give them the slip. She paused and glanced around the Investigations office to see if she was alone. There were two other investigators like Dan, but each was on the phone and didn't seem to notice her.

"There's something else. Chase insists Ariel was killed by a witchfinder."

"Really? Wow. Does he have proof?"

"I don't know yet. We'll see what he says during the interview. I mean, I didn't think witchfinders existed anymore."

"There have been a few cases that I know of, but we never labeled them as such."

"How did you label them?" Charlie asked.

"As serial killers." Ben's voice dropped half an octave to the most serious tone she'd ever heard him use.

Charlie stood straight up, the shock of that news like a poker in her back. "Are you kidding me?"

"No. The thing is the men we've caught have just been murderers obsessed with witches."

"Oh, my goddess. Really?" Charlie's free hand drifted to her throat.

"Yeah."

"So what happens when we catch one?"

"They're rarely a witch, so we hand them over to the local authorities."

"Well, if that's how this turns out, I guess it's a good thing I'm working with the locals."

"You are?"

"Yeah." Charlie sighed. "There's something I have to tell you, and I'm not happy about having to do it, but I think it's in the best interest of the DOL for you to know."

"What is it?"

"When we got here last night, Will immediately went out looking for... you know."

"A vampire's nest." Ben's voice gave away his disappointment.

"Yeah. And that wouldn't be a problem if he was here working with me and the Sheriff's investigator on this case. But he's not. He's holed up in his room. Sleeping it off. I've texted a couple of times and haven't heard from him."

"Okay. I hear you. I'll handle it."

"Thank you. I'm sorry to be a snitch."

"Don't worry about it. I hired him for a job, and if he's not doing it, I need to know that."

"You're not gonna fire him, are you?" Panic crept into her chest.

"No, but I'll talk to him about his priorities."

"Great." Charlie sighed, feeling a little better.

"Are you gonna be okay?"

"Me? Oh yeah. The investigator is a good guy. He gave me a little push back at first, but when I told him I wanted to collaborate, he was open to it. So far we're getting along pretty good."

"I'm glad to hear it. It's a smart move, working with the locals instead of against them."

"I figured it was best since we're not even sure yet if she was murdered."

"Like I said. Smart move. Keep me updated, okay?"

"I will."

Charlie ended the call and stuck her phone in her blazer pocket. The cup felt too cool to steep the tea now, so she topped it off with some more hot water and headed back to the interview room.

Chase straightened up when he recognized her. "Oh, thank goddess. It's you. Can we just get this over with?"

"You have someplace you need to be?" Charlie closed the door behind her and then put the cup of steaming water on the table in front of him.

"No, nothing like that. It's just this situation is so screwed up," he whined. "What is this?" He scowled at the cup of hot water.

"It's water for tea." Charlie pulled out the chair across from him and took a seat.

"I told that cop I didn't want tea." He turned up his nose.

Charlie put the mint tin on the table and pushed it across the table toward him. "You sure about that?"

"What is this?"

"Some teabags I always carry with me. My aunt makes special blends for all occasions."

"Really?" He opened the tin and peered inside. Chase bit his bottom lip and picked up a tea bag.

"That's chamomile, peppermint, and lemon balm."

He held the bag to his nose and drew in a deep breath. His eyes fluttered closed. "Heaven." He plopped the bag into the hot water and let it sink to the bottom of the cup.

"Good choice." Charlie retrieved the sugar and creamer from her pocket and set them next to his cup.

"Thanks," Chase grabbed the packets of sugar, tore them open and dosed his tea. When he was done, he crumpled up the packets and wrapped his hands around the cup.

"So, Chase," Charlie began. She folded her hands

together and leaned forward a little. "How long did you and Ariel date?"

Chase's boyish face deflated, and the corners of his mouth turned down, making him look older. "Two years. She was the one, you know? She totally got me."

"That's a tough loss. I'm really sorry about it."

"Me, too," Chase said.

"When was the last time you saw her?"

"The night before she disappeared. She was going to stay over, but her mom called saying she wasn't feeling well, and she needed Ariel to come home."

"Did her mom say what was wrong with her?"

"No. Sometimes her mom had these sorts of episodes, I guess you'd call them. Depression," he rolled his eyes for a half-second, "and Ariel had to be there to take care of her."

"I see." Charlie nodded, thinking for a moment about Chase's reaction. "Ariel was a good daughter."

"She was. I thought she made it home okay."

"Right. Where was her dad?"

Chase made a scoffing noise. "Bart? Who knows? He was probably at the bar."

"Oh. Did that happen a lot?"

"Oh, yeah. That's why Ariel stayed with me most of the time."

"Right." Charlie scrutinized every wrinkle, every tip

and turn of his head, every blink, trying to suss out his true emotions. She wished for a second that she could still tap into his thoughts. It would make this whole process a lot easier. Since she couldn't do that anymore, maybe it was best if she stopped wishing for it. "So, it's funny. Ariel's mom didn't mention any of that when I talked to her."

"Why would she? It's kind of embarrassing, you know? Nobody in their family talked about it."

Charlie nodded and kept her face as neutral as possible. "One thing she did mention is that you and Ariel wanted to join the DOL."

"Yeah. We were going to. We were working on the applications when this happened."

"When the witchfinder came along?"

"Yeah."

"How did that start exactly?" Charlie asked. "That was a pretty elaborate glamour you put up. Nice work, by the way."

"Thanks," Chase said. He smiled and ducked his head. "She and I did it together, though."

"There were so many elements to it. Is that a natural talent to both of you? Or something you've learned?"

"I'm pretty good at glamours and Ariel picked it up easier than most, although I wouldn't say she was a natural at it."

"The whole thing was definitely impressive."

"Thanks." A prideful smile crossed his lips.

"So, Chase, tell me about the witchfinder."

"Um...it started at Ariel's job. She works..." Pain filled his face, "worked. She worked at a restaurant called Salty Mick's, and this one customer of hers came in all the time. Always wanted to sit in her section. He started asking her questions about whether she was a witch and was witchcraft and magic even real."

"How did she handle that?" Charlie asked.

"Ariel was kind. She answered his questions. Even told him she could introduce him to our High Priestess."

"And did she?" Charlie leaned in more.

"No. She was going to. Had set up a meeting and everything, but he didn't show.

"Then he just stopped coming to the restaurant, and Ariel was happy she didn't have to deal with him anymore. But that's when the letters started, and they freaked her out. Hell, they freaked me out."

"What was in the letters?"

"Just how he didn't want her to be a witch. She was too good for it. Too kind and nice. Stuff like that."

"Were they ever overtly threatening?"

"Only the last one. That's when we put the glamour up, and she tried to change up her routine."

"Did she ever tell her parents or the police?"

"No. Everybody knows the cops won't do anything unless something happens. But by then, it's too late."

"Okay. Do you know where the letters are now? I

know the Sheriff's investigator didn't find any letters. And I didn't find anything, either."

"We used them as part of a banishing spell to make this guy disappear."

"Oh, Chase. Please tell me you just put them in a jar and buried them somewhere."

Chase slouched in his chair and gave her a blank stare. "Um…" his voice trembled. "We burned them."

"Dammit, Chase. That was evidence. His fingerprints could've been on them. Maybe even some DNA."

"We weren't thinking that way. We just wanted him to leave her alone."

"I know. I know." Charlie sat back in her chair and rubbed her fingers through the front of her scalp to calm herself. What the hell had they been thinking? Was Chase even telling the truth? She blew out a heavy breath.

"All right. The letters are gone, right? You did a banishing ritual and burned them. Then what happened?"

"We thought it worked. She didn't get any more letters. But two weeks after we did the banishing ritual, Ariel went missing."

"Why didn't you go to the police when that happened?"

"Because Juniper told me they would look at me first

because I was her boyfriend. She said she wanted to protect me."

"Did you tell her about the letters? About this guy?"

"Yes, I did. I thought she would tell the police, but I guess she didn't."

"No, she didn't." Charlie scowled. Why hadn't Juniper said anything to her about the man stalking her daughter? "Did Juniper believe you when you told her? That this man who was obsessed with her daughter was a witchfinder?"

"Yeah, she did."

Charlie locked her gaze on Chase's. "Are you sure about that? Because she never mentioned it to me. Or to Detective Blankenship."

"She believed me. But you don't, right? You don't believe me?"

"At this point, I don't know what to believe. I need a minute to confer with my partner." Charlie flattened her hands on the table and pushed herself to her feet. "You just stay put. I'll be back."

"Right. Where am I gonna go? He's after me, too." Chase spun his cup in his hands and didn't look at her.

Charlie left the interrogation room and leaned with her back against the door, trying to decide what to do next. Dan's heavy footsteps gave away his approach, and she looked up.

"What the hell?" Dan said.

"I know, right?" Charlie held her hands up in surrender.

"Burning evidence is pretty bad."

"I'm more concerned about whether or not anything he's said is the truth," Charlie said.

"What do you want to do?"

"What I want to do is talk to Juniper Martin again and this High Priestess to confirm his story."

"I think that's a good idea."

"How long can we hold him?"

"Twenty-four hours if the ME doesn't rule it murder, which she won't at this point."

"How long could we hold him if it was ruled a murder?" Charlie asked.

"Without arresting him? Seventy-two hours max."

"Okay." The wheels of Charlie's mind spun over the pieces of the puzzle. Maybe she could get the DOL lab to put a rush on the samples once they got them. "Let me see what I can do."

"So, you want to go back and question the mother again?"

"Yep. I sure do. We'll just let him hang tight here for now if that's okay," Charlie said.

"Perfectly okay."

"Great. Silly me, I thought this was gonna be a short day."

"Yeah, those are always the longest," Dan said.

"Yep," Charlie agreed. "Do you wanna grab a quick bite to eat then head over to the Martins again? I'll buy."

"Deal," Dan said. "I just need to let my commander know what we're doing so that our good buddy Chase doesn't try to run again."

"Sure. But I don't think he's going anywhere. I think he really does believe someone is after him, and as long as he feels safe here, he will stay locked in that room."

"Good. You like burgers? I'll take you to the best burger joint in town."

"Sounds great."

"Okay, I'll meet you at the front after I talk to my commander."

CHAPTER 16

Dan led Juniper Martin down the corridor toward Interview Room Two. Charlie waited in the room with Chase, listening for the signal. She and Dan had agreed he would raise his voice a little in the hall and thank Juniper for coming with them to the station to answer more questions.

When Charlie heard the magic words, she opened the door wide enough that Juniper could look inside and see Chase Andrews.

Charlie turned her attention to Chase. "Is there anything I can get you?"

"A cushion for my ass would be nice." He bounced a little in his seat, his shirt hanging open at the collar and his thin sandy colored hair looked oily as if he'd scrubbed his hands through his hair too many times. A five o'clock shadow darkened the lower part of his face, and the skin beneath his eyes looked almost bruised. "These chairs are super uncomfortable."

Charlie nodded. "I'll see what I can do. I'll be back in a little bit."

Dan slowed down just long enough to give Juniper a chance to peer into the room. Charlie smiled at the woman and pulled the door shut behind her.

"Hi, Juniper," Charlie chirped. "Thank you so much for coming down to talk to us. I know it's getting late in the day. Hopefully, we'll be able to wrap this up quickly."

"Anything I can do to help." Juniper's gaze darted toward the door behind Charlie. She pushed her curly salt and pepper hair behind one ear. A dangling silver pentacle earring winked in the overhead light. "So, was that Chase Andrews?" She hiked her hand-woven purse over her shoulder, holding onto it as if it were a lifeline. She gave Charlie a worried glance.

"Um..." Charlie jerked her thumb to the door behind her. "We're in the process of interviewing him. It's been very informative." She smiled and deferred back to Dan. "I'll let Dan get you settled. Can I get you anything to drink? Coffee, soda, hot tea?"

"Some hot tea would be nice," she said.

"Sure thing." Charlie exchanged a glance with Dan, and he pulled himself up tall, emanating a quiet authority. He extended his hand toward the coffee station, and Charlie took the cue and headed off.

"Right this way, Ms. Martin," he said, ushering her down the hall toward the open interview room.

At the coffee station, Charlie filled a paper cup with hot water. She grabbed a couple of packs of sugar, one of the packaged teabags, and a small creamer cup, and headed toward the interview room. In her heart, she didn't think Juniper Martin could've killed her daughter. Mother's rarely killed their children. But there were holes in Juniper's story that needed filling.

Charlie walked inside and put the cup down on the table in front of Juniper, then placed the teabag, sugar, and creamer on the table next to it.

"Here you go. Dan, can I see you for just a minute?"

"Sure," Dan said. Juniper ripped open the teabag and put it into the cup. Charlie held the door open until Dan passed through and closed it behind her.

"What's up?" Dan asked.

"Chase is complaining about the chair. It's uncomfortable. Which I can vouch for."

Dan's brows knitted together, and he nodded. "Okay. Give me a second." Dan disappeared down the hall and turned into the cubicle area. He returned pushing an office chair on wheels with a padded seat and back. "This should do it."

"Great." Charlie took control of the chair and pushed

it into the interview room. "Will this do?" she asked Chase.

"Oh, goddess, yes." Chase popped up from the hard plastic and metal chair, relief in his voice. He stood up and stretched his back, walked around the table a few times, and then dramatically pulled the chair to the table and sat down.

"Oh, yes. Yes. Yes. Yes." He closed his eyes as if he'd just sunk into a cloud. "So much better. Those plastic chairs are practically torture devices."

"I couldn't agree more," Charlie said. "So, you're good for now?"

"Yes. Thank you."

"No problem. I'll be back in a little bit."

"Any chance I could get some food?" Chase asked.

Charlie shrugged. "I'll see what I can do."

"Great. Thanks." He leaned forward, folded his arms, and laid his head down in the crook of one of his elbows. Charlie cocked her head. Chase had gotten awfully comfortable here, and she didn't know what to make of that just yet. She tucked the thought away and left him alone to nap.

A few moments later, she joined Dan in interview room two. She took a seat in the chair next to him and tried not to frown at the feel of the hard plastic on her backside.

"How's your tea?" Charlie asked, nodding at Juniper.

Juniper blew on the steaming cup of liquid and took a sip. "Good. Thanks."

Charlie glanced at Dan and signaled she was ready.

"So, Juniper, we just had a few more questions for you," Dan began.

Juniper looked up over the top of her cup. "Uh-huh."

"Yeah, so, we were talking to Chase, and he mentioned that the night Ariel went missing, she was supposed to come home and take care of you. Is that true?"

Juniper blinked her eyes several times before answering. "Yeah. That's probably true. I don't really remember."

"Did Ariel take care of you a lot?" Dan asked.

"I relied on my daughter. That's why she lived at home. That's not a secret. Did Chase tell you it was?"

Dan's face gave nothing away. "It's just kind of funny because when I talked to you and Bart two weeks ago, y'all didn't say anything about why she lived at home or that she helped take care of you when you were..." He paused as if he was trying to find the right word. "When you were not feeling well. I do remember you being upset because Ariel didn't come home. But you pretty much lied to me when I asked if she had a boyfriend and if she stayed at his house a lot."

"Is that what Chase told you?" Juniper straightened in her chair, an indignant look on her face. "She did not stay there all the time. Only a couple of nights a week at most."

"Sure. But still. You lied about her having a boyfriend at all. So..."

Juniper eyed Dan from beneath her dark brows. Her lips pressed into a straight line.

"It makes me wonder. If you didn't tell us the truth about her boyfriend, then what else aren't you telling us?" Dan asked.

Charlie studied Juniper's face. Studied the way she squirmed in her seat and tightened her narrow jaw.

"Juniper, where was your husband during all this? Why wasn't he there to take care of you?" Charlie asked.

Juniper scowled and gave Charlie the kind of look she knew well. A death glare. Charlie kept a neutral face, trying not to let on how pleased she was that she must've hit a nerve.

"So, Chase didn't tell you?"

"Tell us what?" Dan asked.

"Bart and I are separated. He's been living with this little tramp who joined our coven about a year ago. I suffer from depression, and it can be very debilitating. So, you see, I needed Ariel to help me when I was having a hard time getting out of bed."

"I'm so sorry," Charlie said. She locked eyes with Juniper. "I know what that's like. I've had bouts of depression myself."

"Thank you. It is hard. I don't know what I'm going to do without Ariel." Juniper sniffled and wiped at the corner of her eye. Were there tears there? Charlie couldn't be sure. Juniper's eyes didn't look wet or teary.

"Then it must've been upsetting when Ariel told you that she and Chase were going to leave Florida and go work for the DOL."

Juniper's death glare resurfaced. "I couldn't stand in the way of what my daughter wanted."

"It's hard being a mom. You want what's best for your kids. But they have other ideas about what they want. Letting go? I think that's probably the hardest thing any mom can do. I know it is for me sometimes."

"Exactly. I was torn. Because I needed her, and she was going to leave me." Juniper's voice quivered.

"Let me ask you a question." Charlie leaned forward in her chair. "Did you and Ariel have a fight the night she went missing? About her leaving?"

Juniper rolled her eyes. "She was my daughter. I'm her mother. Sometimes we fought. It didn't mean anything."

"Right, but what about that night?" Charlie pushed harder.

"I don't remember," Juniper said.

"Why is that? Were you medicated or maybe drinking?" Dan asked.

"I took some Valerian root and went to bed." Juniper folded her arms across her chest and sat back as far as she could in her chair.

"Not Belladonna?" Charlie asked.

"No. I don't use Belladonna. It's too easy to use too much," Juniper insisted. "Why are you asking me about Belladonna?"

"I'm just curious, that's all. It's a common sedative in our community," Charlie said. "And I know how poisonous it can be if you don't get the dosage right."

"Is that what killed Ariel?" Juniper lifted a hand to her throat, a look of horror on her face.

"It's on our radar." Charlie laced her fingers together. "We're still waiting on results from the medical examiner."

"Like I said, I don't even keep it in my house. You are welcome to go and check." Juniper flashed her palm at Charlie.

"We'll do that," Dan said.

"Let's go back to before Ariel went missing. Did she ever mention that someone was stalking her?" Charlie asked.

"Not exactly. She did mention that some customer at work had become infatuated with her. That he'd sent her some weird letters. But she didn't say who he was or that he was stalking her."

"Did you see the letters? Or encourage her to report it to her boss or the police?" Charlie couldn't help but imagine Evan in a similar situation. And if Evan had received letters like Chase had described, there would be no stopping her from getting to the bottom of it. No matter how old he was.

"I saw them very briefly in her room when I was dusting. She accused me of going through her things. But that's not what I was doing. I swear. They were lying on top of her books next to her bed."

"Really?" Charlie asked. "She just left them lying around?"

"Okay, they weren't really on top of her books. They were folded up inside one, but I accidentally knocked the stack over when I was cleaning. The book fell on the floor, and the letters flew out."

"And you read them?" Charlie leaned in.

"Only a little bit. Ariel came in, and that's when we fought. Then she went to Chase's and..." She sniffled; her dark eyes glassy with real tears this time. "I never saw her again."

"She didn't come home after that?" Charlie asked.

"No. I begged her to. It even sent me into one of my spells. This is all my fault. If I hadn't asked her to come take care of me..."

"Juniper, you didn't do this," Charlie said. From the corner of her eye she saw Dan turn his head and stare at her with a look of confusion on his face. Charlie ignored him. "I know this is hard. But we want the same thing. We want to find out what happened to Ariel."

"Yes..." Juniper whispered. "I just want her to be at peace."

"Me too," Charlie said. "Is there any chance you saw the word witchfinder in those letters?"

"I don't..." Juniper shook her head. "I wish..." She closed her eyes. "I remember they seemed threatening. But when I asked her about that, she told me not to worry about it. She said it was just a joke."

"How come you didn't mention those letters to us when you filed the missing person's report?" Dan said.

"I was so scared I couldn't think straight. And she'd told me not to worry."

"She probably did that a lot didn't she?" Charlie said.

"Yeah, she did."

Charlie considered Juniper's interpretation, and she drew parallels to her own life during that dark time when she was so depressed. How many times had Evan, who was just a little boy at the time, put on a brave face for her? How many times had he downplayed his own troubles so he wouldn't burden her? She couldn't deny the words rang true. Maybe Ariel just didn't want to upset her depressed mother.

"Would she have talked to anyone else about them? Besides Chase?" Charlie asked.

"She might've told our High Priestess. They were close." Juniper shifted in her chair. "I gave you her name and number before. Remember?"

"Of course. She's next on my list to talk to." Charlie

exchanged glances with Dan. "Do you have any other questions?"

"Um. Yeah," Dan said, shifting in his seat and leaning forward. "Would you mind giving us your husband's phone number? We'd like to cover all our bases."

"Of course," Juniper said.

"Great. We'll be back in a few minutes," Charlie said. She stood up, and Dan rose to his feet, then the two of them left Juniper to finish her tea. They walked back to Dan's cubicle in silence. Dan leaned against the edge of his desk and gestured for Charlie to take a seat in his padded office chair.

"So, what do you think?" Dan asked.

"I don't know what I think. I can tell you what I feel. And even that's not based on anything other than good old-fashioned intuition."

"Let's hear it," Dan said.

"Honestly, I don't think Juniper could've killed her daughter. I think she needed her too much."

"Even though she was leaving her for that job?"

"It could be motive, and I could be totally wrong..." Charlie began. She wished more than anything, she could've read Juniper's thoughts. Relying on her intuition scared her. What if she got it wrong? "I don't think she did it. And that said, we really need to stay on top of the ME for lab results and check her house. Can you send a forensic tech to go through her cupboards?"

"Or you and I can do it when we take her home."

"Okay. That sounds good."

"Now what about Chase?"

"Chase is scared out of his gourd. That illusion he and Ariel created was the most elaborate I've ever seen. You don't spend that much time and energy on something unless you really don't want to be found. And..." Charlie shook her head. "I just don't see any motive. She was going to leave with him. They were going to build a new life together. Why would he kill her?"

"All good points." Dan scrubbed the back of his head. "That takes us back to square one."

"Yeah, I know. Why don't we let them go? We'll go check her cupboards and if we find anything, we'll bring her back in. I don't think either of them is gonna go anywhere. In fact, I think Chase may just request we hold him."

"Yeah, I can't do that unless he's a viable suspect," Dan said.

"I know," Charlie said.

"Let's go break the bad news to him. We can drive them home, check her house, and I'll drop you off at your hotel."

"Sounds like a plan," Charlie said.

CHAPTER 17

Dan pulled up to the front door of the Holiday Inn Express. Charlie let out a deep breath, looking forward to changing out of her clothes, ordering food, and watching mindless television. Her muscles protested when she attempted to move. She stared at the welcoming yellow light of the double doors of the hotel.

"This has been one long day," Charlie mused. "And it's not over yet."

"How's that?" Dan asked.

"Because now I have to go deal with my partner," she said.

"Man, I don't envy you that," Dan said.

Charlie shifted her gaze from the door to Dan and

gave him a grateful smile. "Despite my partner's absence, this case has turned out to be an interesting challenge. I've really enjoyed working with you."

"You say that like the case is closed," Dan teased. "Of course, it might be for you. We might be dealing with a good, old-fashioned murderer."

"Maybe so. But working with you has made it a lot easier."

"I have to admit that working with you has definitely been eye-opening. And a bit fun. You're a good investigator."

"I appreciate that. So are you."

"You sure you don't want to grab some take-out?"

"Naw, I'll just order a pizza or something. I'll be fine."

"All righty then. I won't keep you. I'm bushed. I haven't had a partner with as much energy as you in I can't remember when."

He grinned and reached into the front breast pocket of his polo shirt and retrieved a business card with the Sheriff's department logo on it.

"Give me a call in the morning, and I'll pick you up. We can go talk to that priestess lady."

"Great." Charlie took the card and scanned it briefly before tucking it into the outer pocket of her purse.

"The second number is my cell."

"Is it okay if I text you instead of calling?"

"Of course." Dan nodded and smiled.

"Wonderful. I'll see you in the morning then." Charlie climbed out of the Tahoe and dragged herself through the lobby to the hall where the elevators would take her to the third floor. Halfway between the first and third floors, she wished she had looked in the parking lot for Will's car. Hopefully he had gotten his fill of vampires last night and was lazing about in his room. She thought carefully about what she would say. Even though she didn't know Will very well and her psychic abilities were, for the most part, out of commission, something was going on with him.

She understood Will's need to be secretive and he didn't strike her as the most touchy-feely kind of guy. She went over what she wanted to say to him in her head on the trip up. She didn't want to hurt his feelings if he *was* going through something. But at the same time, she needed him to do his job. To be her partner. The elevator stopped on her floor and a couple of minutes later she found herself standing in front of Will's door. She pressed her hand against her stomach. The Do Not Disturb sign was still in the lock, and the sight of it irritated her. She knocked hard on the door and waited for an answer, for any sign that he might be inside. She heard nothing.

"You have got to be kidding me," she muttered. She glanced one way and then the other down the hall before pulling her wand from her purse. She gripped it tightly, focusing her energy, and whispered, "Unlock, unlock, unlock." Once she heard the mechanism click, Charlie pressed the handle down and pushed against the door.

"Will? Are you in here?" She passed the dark bathroom letting the door close behind her. Everything in the kitchenette looked in order as if no one had used it.

"It's me, Charlie. I really need to talk to you."

She stepped around the corner and stared at the two empty queen beds. Neither one looked slept in or even rumpled. Charlie looked around for the duffel bag Will had carried when they checked in. She found it in the closet and unzipped it. It held his clothes and toiletry bag. Had he even come back last night?

"Dammit, Will." Charlie retrieved her phone from her bag and dialed Ben's number.

"Charlie," Ben said, sounding a little too overjoyed. "We were just talking about you."

Friday night dinner. A wave of homesickness hit her right in the gut, and Charlie sat down on the edge of the bed, just listening for a second to her cousins chattering over each other, Evangeline scolding them and Jason making a smart-ass remark that made them all laugh. Her eyes welled with tears, and a pebble formed in her throat, making it impossible to speak.

"Charlie?" Ben asked.

Charlie swallowed the emotion and cleared her

throat. "I'm here. I should've known y'all were talking about me."

"Were your ears burning?" Ben said.

"Not quite." She blinked back the tears and got herself under control. "Listen, I need to talk to you, seriously. Can you step out onto the porch, please?"

"Sure," Ben said.

In the background, Charlie heard her aunt's voice, "Don't be too long, Ben, supper's almost ready," and a fresh wave of emotion washed through her. She rested her elbow on her knee and held her forehead with her free hand.

"Okay, I'm outside. What's up? You okay?" Ben asked.

"I'm fine. More than fine. We're still spinning our wheels a bit on the case, but that's not why I'm calling you."

"Let me guess. It's Will," Ben said. "I left him a message to call me."

"Okay, but I still haven't heard from him. I let myself into his room, and it doesn't even look like he's been here at all. I don't think he came home last night. I'm really getting worried."

"Will's been hunting vamps a long time. He can take care of himself."

"Normally, I'd agree, but we're in a strange city, and I don't even know where to begin to look for him."

"He didn't give you the address he was going to?" Ben asked, the first sign of concern edging into his voice.

"Wait. Yes, he did. He texted it to me. I forgot."

"Okay." She could hear him pacing around the back porch of her uncle's house. "Let me try calling him again. Maybe he's just being—"

"A jerk?" Charlie chimed in.

"Something like that. I'll call you right back."

"Thank you," Charlie said. "I really appreciate it."

Charlie put the phone down on the bed next to her and waited. The longer it took for Ben to call her back, the tighter the knot in her stomach wound. She rose to her feet and paced back and forth in front of the bed. Maybe Ben had gotten hold of Will and was reading him the riot act. He certainly deserved it after everything he'd put them through.

Her phone chirped, signaling she had a text. She quickly picked it up and opened her messaging app. The name at the top read Will Tucker. Her heart leaped for a minute. Finally! He was texting her back. Maybe Ben *had* gotten through to him.

When she took a good look at what appeared on the screen, her stomach roiled. Hot bile raced up her throat, and she sprinted to the bathroom, making it just in time to retch. When she finished emptying her stomach, she grabbed a clean towel and wiped her mouth.

It took a second to gather the strength to look at the

photo again. When she did, she studied the picture. There was no way to identify who was in the photo. The splotchy marbled skin of the torso glowed almost white because of the flash from the phone. Whoever it was had been split from breastbone to navel and opened wide. What was left of his entrails and organs had been displayed on his chest.

Charlie considered every detail of the image, trying to find any indication that this could be Will. Something inside her, some deep intuition, told her it couldn't be him.

What had Will told her? Sometimes vampires kept their victims for days to feast on the organs. The skin looked too gray, too marbled for it to be him. In her work with Jason Tate, she'd seen her share of decayed bodies. Even if they had killed Will last night, his skin wouldn't be this color yet. A spark of hope lit her heart.

The phone chirped and vibrated in her hand when another text came through. This time a video was attached. Her finger shook a little when she held it above the arrow within a circle. She swallowed hard and pressed the arrow, and the video started.

"Good evening, witch," a familiar voice purred. The shaky video moved around before finally focusing on Will tied to a chair. He looked pallid in the harsh light of the constant flash illuminating his body. He wore no shirt, and there appeared to be bite marks in his neck and along his arms and wrists on both sides. "Are you missing your partner? He's been waiting for you all night and all day."

"Don't believe him, Charlie." Will looked up at the camera. He still had a little fight left in his eyes. "Do not fall for his bullshit."

"He's been a delicious appetizer so far, but we've been saving our appetite for something a little sweeter."

"Charlie, stay away!" Despite his bravado, Will sounded weak and tired.

The vampire flipped the camera quickly. The speed of it made Charlie dizzy for a moment. The camera steadied on the vampire's face when he held it at arm's length.

"Do you remember me? I know your name, Charlie. Do you know mine?" He chuckled. "Come and get me. The clock is ticking for your partner."

"You son of a bitch," Charlie whispered. How could she forget the vampire who'd gotten away from them the other night? His twisted ugly face was etched in her mind. "I will kill you."

"I'll send you the address. Can't wait to see you, Charlie." The vampire pressed his fingers to his mouth and blew her a kiss. The video ended.

Charlie dialed Ben's number immediately, and he picked up on the first ring. "Charlie, I haven't gotten an answer yet."

"I just got a video from the vampire that got away

from us the other night. He has Will." Her throat closed, and panic threatened to choke her.

"What?"

"Yeah. He wants me."

"No, Charlie, don't fall for it," Ben said.

"They will kill him, Ben. I can't let that happen."

"Fine, all right. I'll give you that. But you can't do this alone. I'll be on the road in half an hour. Wait for me, and we'll face the nest together."

"I don't know if I can do that. I'm sorry, Ben."

"Charlie. What about Evan?"

"This vampire wants me. Do you think Evan will ever be safe if that creature is still alive? No. I'm ending this tonight."

"Charlie wait—"

Charlie ended the call and closed her eyes. She didn't want to go against Ben, but what choice did she have? If she waited, Will would die. She took a deep breath and fished Dan's card out of her purse, then dialed his number.

"Hey, Dan, it's Charlie. I'm sorry to bother you. I know our day just ended, but I could really use your help."

"What's going on?" Dan said.

"My partner's been kidnapped."

"Are you sure?" Dan said, his voice full of concern.

"Yeah, they sent me a video."

"Maybe we should get the FBI involved. I've got a buddy—"

"That will take too long," Charlie said. "And I don't really think they're equipped to deal with these particular kidnappers."

"Oh-kay. I'm not sure what that means."

"My partner sometimes hunts vampires."

Dan laughed, but there was no humor in the sound, only nervous energy and incredulity. "Oh shit. Are you kidding me?"

"No. Vampires are a real thing, and there's evidently a nest in an old warehouse that he went after last night. They have him," Charlie said. Dan grew quiet, and for a second, Charlie thought she'd lost him. "You still there?"

"Yeah, I'm here. Can they be killed?" Dan asked, determination in his voice.

"Yes."

"All right. I'll pick you up."

"Thank you, Dan," Charlie said. "I know all this is overwhelming and a bit crazy."

"And I'm assuming dangerous?"

"Yes. Bring every weapon you have and extra ammunition if you have it."

"Oh, I have it. Don't you worry. Can they be killed with bullets?"

"I don't really know. You have to chop off their heads

to kill them so my guess is, if you shoot them in the head it could do the same thing."

"Good. I'll be there in twenty."

"I'll be out front." Charlie ended the call and went to her room to change clothes and gather what tools she had with her that might help her get Will out of this mess alive.

CHAPTER 18

"Are you sure this is the right address?"

"Yep. This is it," Charlie said when Dan pulled up to the warehouse. He parked on the street and examined the site. A tall chain-link fence surrounded the building with No Trespassing signs tacked on every hundred feet. A heavy chain wrapped around the gate, secured by a huge padlock.

Just down the street, Charlie spotted Will's Mustang. "That's Will's car."

She climbed out of the Tahoe and stared at the building for a moment. Even without her psychic abilities, she could feel dark energy emanating from the walls and windows. She noticed a red sticker on the window of the front door.

Dan moved to the back of the truck and opened the

rear door with his remote. Charlie joined him. In the dim light glow of the interior light, she watched him put on a bulletproof vest and a tactical vest with a patch on it that read Sheriff in white letters.

He loaded the pockets with extra magazines of ammunition for his weapon and shells for a shotgun. Then he checked the weapon on his hip and unlocked a rack installed along the inside of the Tahoe's back cabin. He grabbed an oily mean-looking shotgun, opened it, and dropped five shells into the chambers.

"What does that red sticker mean?" Charlie pointed toward the front door of the warehouse.

"It means this building is condemned. Probably damaged in the last hurricane."

"Figures," she muttered.

"You know, I'd really feel better if you'd wear this." He took an extra vest from the stockpile of paraphernalia in the back and handed it to her.

"Are you planning to shoot me?" She held it in her hands and felt the weight of it. "It's lighter than it looks."

"I just don't want either of us to get hurt."

Charlie laid the vest down in the back of the truck. "I'm more worried about their teeth and their speed than I am about getting shot. But I appreciate the sentiment. And for the record, I don't want us to get hurt, either." She sighed and faced him. "You can still back out if you want.

This is gonna be bloody and stinky and probably the worst thing you've ever encountered."

"I did two tours in Iraq. I can handle this." He placed a beefy hand on her shoulder and gave it a squeeze. The kindness in his smile belied a steely insistence in his demeanor. She pictured him in charge of his men during the war, his air of authority giving them confidence, daring them to brook his orders. She wasn't going to talk Dan out of anything.

"Okay." She nodded in the direction of the street. "Let's go break into Will's trunk. There's stuff in there we'll need."

"Lead the way." Dan gestured for her to go first and pressed the button on his remote. The liftgate lowered on its own, and he followed her to Will's Mustang, holding his shotgun loosely in his hand.

Charlie pulled her wand from her purse and pressed the tip of it to the lock on the trunk of Will's car. "Unlock, unlock, unlock," she said in a low voice. The mechanism clicked, and the trunk lid popped open. Charlie flipped on the jimmy-rigged lighting system and examined all the options for killing vampires.

"Holy shit, is that a Katana?" Dan asked.

"I think so."

"Da-yum." Dan pulled the long, curved-bladed sword from its foam holder and held it up. "I've always wanted to use one of these."

"Right." Charlie took the sword out of his hands. "I promise you'll be better off with one of these." She put a machete in his hand and put the sword back into its holder. Dan checked out the blade with his thumb.

"At least it's sharp."

"Careful, don't cut yourself. We don't want to rile them up any more than they already are with the smell of your blood."

Dan nodded. "Good point."

Charlie took a machete for herself and stuck it inside her purse then rearranged the bag so it hung across her body.

"I just need to do one quick thing," she said and quickly jotted off a text to her son.

Hey, Sweetie. Just wanted to tell you how much I love you.

A few seconds later, he responded.

I love you too, Mom. You okay?

Yep. Evangeline is going to pick you up Sunday. You be good and listen to her.

I will.

Charlie tasted salt in the back of her throat and blinked back the sudden tears that blurred her vision. She switched contacts and made a quick text to Ben.

Sorry I couldn't wait. Tell Evangeline and the rest of the family I love them, and I'm sorry that I've been so distant lately. Take care.

Almost immediately, her phone began to buzz in her

hands. Ben's name appeared on the screen. Charlie ignored the call and put the phone on silent mode. She slipped her phone into her bag and spotted a box of bandanas in the back of the trunk. She grabbed two of the scarves, held them to her nose and gave them a sniff. The heavy scents of rosemary, clove, and lemon made her cough. She sniffled and handed one to Dan. "Take this and wrap it around your face."

"Why?" He gave it a sniff and his nose wrinkled.

"It'll help mask the smell. Vampires reek of decay and death. You saw the video. They've got at least one dead body in there."

Dan nodded and stuffed the bandana into one of the pockets of his tactical vest. "Maybe later."

Charlie shrugged and slammed the trunk lid closed. "Suit yourself."

They approached the gate, and Charlie didn't waste any time unlocking the padlock with her wand. Once it opened, she lifted the heavy lock off the chains and let it drop to the ground. Dan unwrapped the chain, and they walked across the ruins of the gravel and asphalt parking lot like two gunslingers headed to a showdown.

The window of the metal door to the right of a huge garage door was covered with some sort of black paper.

"Is that to keep them from bursting into flames in the sunlight?" Dan pointed to the blackened window.

"No. That's a myth. But their eyes are sensitive to

light." She touched the tip of her wand to the dingy metal door handle and whispered her unlocking spell. The lock clicked, and she winced at the screech of the rusty hinges when she opened the door. The air chilled her skin despite the sixty-five-degree temperature outside. Something brushed across the back of her neck, and she jumped. She held up her wand, and the tip glowed a bright white. She held it in the direction of whatever it was that touched her and found ragged spider webs hanging from the low ceiling. She quickly brushed her fingers across her hair and scraped away any of the sticky webbing. Her nose wrinkled in disgust, and she wiped the debris on her jeans.

The soft, muffled sounds of movement drew her attention to the door leading into the warehouse. The sickening stench of rotting flesh drifted through her senses, and she quickly tied the bandana around her head to cover her nose and mouth. Dan followed her lead and tied on his bandana. Charlie murmured the word, "Brighter." The tip of her wand cast a wide umbrella of light around them and allowed her to meet Dan's wide eyes.

"Ready?" she whispered. Dan lifted the butt of his shotgun to his shoulder and nodded. "Remember to aim for the head." A soft moaning beckoned to her. "Will," she whispered.

The two of them entered the dark, cavernous warehouse, and she forced the light from her wand to grow even brighter.

Her breath caught in her throat at the sight of fifty pairs of eyes glowing like silver coins in the darkness. Charlie's heart slammed against her ribcage.

"Sweet baby Jesus," Dan muttered.

Charlie let out a ragged breath and began to swirl the tip of her wand in small circles.

Circle of light surrounding me,
Circle of light, Unbreakable be.

A blue circle lifted from the tip like a bright glowing smoke ring and settled around Charlie and Dan.

"Just stay with me, Dan," she said and pressed her back against him. A chorus of grunts and loud growls echoed around them. Charlie shined the light from her wand to the center of the warehouse. She could make out two dark shapes. One standing and one sitting.

"Will? Is that you?"

"I told you not to come," Will groaned.

"Yeah, like that would happen," she snapped. "Just hang on, okay?"

A rustling sound drew her attention away for a second, and she almost dropped her wand at the sight of the vampire rushing toward her. Without much thought, she whispered, "With this light, I stun thee into stillness."

A bolt of light shot from her wand and struck the vampire in the chest. He flew back a few feet and landed on his back as though he's been zapped by a super-powerful Taser. One of his legs twitched, but he didn't get up. She may have lost her psychic powers, but her magic was as strong as ever.

A deafening shot rang out behind her, and she took a step away from Dan's back. She turned quickly to find him pumping the shotgun. The shell casing ejected, spitting outside the smokey circle encasing them. Charlie's ears rang like she'd been standing next to a speaker at a concert, but she saw the vampire's still corpse sprawled on the ground outside the circle, his face shredded by the shotgun blast. At least she'd been right about aiming for the head. She fought the urge to vomit and looked away. She pressed her back against Dan's again. Heat radiated off him, but his sweat-soaked shirt felt wet against her skin.

"We need to move," she whispered. Dan responded, but his words sounded muffled like he was talking to her underwater. She took a sidestep toward Will and the vampire guarding him. From the corner of her eye, she saw the other vampires circling them, drawing closer with each orbit around them. The ringing in her ear from the gunshot dimmed enough that she could finally hear them and see them. Panic flooded her chest. What the hell did she think she was doing?

When they were close enough to the vampire guarding Will, she recognized the ugly son of a bitch. The vampire that had escaped during the nest cleaning in Garnersville. It had only been two days, but it seemed like a lifetime ago now.

"You," she spat the word.

"Yes, me, witch. Did you think I wouldn't make you both pay? You took my family from me," he said.

"Yes, well, I'm sure you took them from their families," Charlie said. "Now let him go, and I won't kill you slowly."

The vampire's cackle grated her nerves. "I'd like to see you try."

"Oh, I will kill you. Trust me."

"I thought all you witches revered nature and her divine order."

"There's nothing natural about you."

"Charlie, please..." Will pleaded. "Get out of here. I'm not worth you dying."

"I am not leaving you!"

One of the vampires rushed them, and Charlie stunned it. Then another and another. Dan got off four more deafening shots. Charlie managed to edge them closer to Will.

The first vampire Charlie shot got to his feet and joined his brothers and sisters. Then other wounded vampires began to recover.

"Shit," she mumbled and aimed her wand to shoot at them again. More of them rushed the circle, and Charlie couldn't keep up. Some hit the boundary and were thrown back, but that only seemed to make them angrier and more determined to get through.

"Yes, yes my brothers and sisters. They cannot stay protected forever." The ringleader grabbed Will and jerked him to his feet. He ripped the skin off his skinny vampire wrist with his teeth and held the bleeding arm to Will's mouth. Will struggled at first, blood smearing across his face. But then he grabbed the vampire's arm and began to drink in earnest.

"Will, no!" Charlie screamed, stepping to the edge of the boundary. "Don't drink." She took aim at the vile creature and shot at his head. He pivoted, putting Will into the line of fire. The spell struck Will in the chest. He stopped drinking and crumpled to the ground. The vampire growled and quickly melted into the shadows.

"Charlie, what do we do?" Dan cast his shotgun to the ground, then pulled his handgun from its holster and shot another vampire in the head.

One of the vampires walked up to the circle and screeched at the top of his lungs, pushing his hand into the circle. His feet moved back a few steps, but he dug into the concrete floor fighting the spell.

Charlie screamed and hit it in the chest, but the wand didn't work. In that moment, the circle around them vanished, and the remaining vampires descended on them. One of the vampires knocked Charlie to the ground and pinned her down. He slammed her right hand with the wand hard against the concrete floor until she heard something crack. The wand slipped from her grasp as sharp pain shot up her arm like liquid fire. Her other hand found the flesh of the creature's face, and she dug her fingernails into its cheek.

It screeched, and she held the vampire inches away from her face with her forearm to his neck. His hot breath reeked of coppery blood and rotten meat. In the fury of the fight, she had lost track of Will and Dan. Had Will been turned? She wasn't sure, just as she didn't know if Dan had been taken down and killed.

"Tom! I need you," she screamed into the face of the vampire.

Within the space of a minute, Tom's reaper form materialized from the darkness. He lifted the vampire off her with such ease it shocked her. In one stroke of his scythe, the vampire's head came away from his body and rolled into the darkness. Tom attacked the vampires that stayed to fight, slicing through them like they were stalks of wheat. Most of them skittered away into the shadows to escape his blade.

Charlie crawled toward Will, cradling her hand against her chest and breathing deeply over the sharp jabs of pain shooting up her arm. She managed to turn him on his back. His eyes fluttered open.

"I told you not to come," he whispered.

A hand touched her shoulder, and she jerked away from it.

"It's all right. It's just me," Tom said. Charlie turned and found him with his hands up. "I won't hurt you."

"They made him drink blood." Charlie's voice quivered. "I don't know what to do."

"First thing we need to do is get all of you to a hospital." Tom knelt beside her, his warm hand extended, and he held out her wand. "You're hurt."

Charlie blinked at him and took the wand with her left hand. She lit the tip and scanned the warehouse. All the vampires were either dead or gone. A few feet away, she found Dan on his knees but still upright. He sat back on his haunches, his arms covered in bites, his gun still in his hand.

"Dan? Are you okay?"

"Yeah." He eyed Tom. "But when this is all said and done, you've got some 'splainin' to do, Charlie."

Charlie nodded and gave him a weary smile. "Yes, I do," she said and turned to meet Tom's steady gaze. "I do have some explaining to do."

CHAPTER 19

"Charlie, you cannot drive." Tom followed Charlie out of the warehouse, but she ignored him, cradling her arm and continuing down the street to Will's car.

"Fine," she snapped, more exhausted than angry. "Then you drive." She felt her way around the back wheel well until she found the magnetic box with the key and handed it over to him.

The ambulances had responded quickly to Dan's 911 call and rushed Will and Dan to emergency to have them typed and cross-matched ASAP. They'd both lost a lot of blood.

She conjured up a spell to cope with the pain on the way to the hospital, but it was wearing off now. She and Tom waited their turn when they arrived, and she tried not to pay too much attention to all the other people waiting in the emergency room of the small hospital.

Tom, sitting beside her now, his arms crossed tightly, said little. Every few minutes, he stole a glance at her. She didn't need psychic abilities to feel his frustration with her. She hadn't answered many of his questions on the drive over and had barely said a word since the receptionist told them to have a seat.

She would tell him everything. Eventually. She swore to herself she would when he'd walked her into the hospital. But not now. Not while Will's future hung over her head like a guillotine waiting to drop. Will would become a vampire, no matter how many transfusions they gave him in the ER, no amount of medical intervention that she knew of could stop the process, not even a total blood replacement. If they could find the sire before Will fed on human blood...maybe.

Charlie broke from her reverie and reached into her bag and dug out her phone. She should at least text Ben to let him know they were still alive. It took her a second to focus on the screen in her hand and she stared at the little messaging app icon, trying to remember what the red circle meant.

"Tom?" she said softly. "What does this mean?" She handed him the phone and pointed to the red circle with the number 15 in the corner. He gave her a worried look.

"You don't know what this means?" he asked.

"I...I can't remember."

"It means you have 15 messages waiting for you to read."

"Oh shit." She took the phone out of his hands. Her heart fluttered, and she let out a sigh and tapped on the app with her good thumb.

"Do you need help?" Tom asked.

"Do I need help?" she muttered. Pain shot up her arm as if someone had jammed it with a hot poker. Every slight movement of her hand brought fresh agony. "I don't know. Probably."

The first message in bold was from Ben. The next three were from Jen, Lisa, and strangely enough, Jason.

Charlie tapped the messages from Ben. The first one begged her not to do this. To wait.

She thumbed down to the last message. It simply read:

We are on our way.

"Oh shit," Charlie said and straightened up in her chair. More pain. She groaned, her arm on fire now.

"What is it?" Tom said.

"Ben's on his way here."

"Good," Tom said. "Maybe he'll know what to do about Will."

"Maybe," she said. "I don't know that there's anything that can be done." Tears stung her eyes. She let this happen. She should've stopped him. Should have

173

appealed to him more about working for the DOL. Should've laid more guilt on him. Anything to make him stop hunting vampires.

"How long will it take them to get here?" Tom asked.

"It took us almost seven hours. And Will is a speed demon."

Tom glanced down at his wrist then showed the screen to her. The large square digital watch that could be paired with his smartphone read 2:40 a.m..

"What time was the last text sent?" She handed him the phone.

He read the screen. "Eight-thirty last night."

Charlie closed her eyes. The last twenty-four hours seemed like a week's worth of living, with little to no time for thinking. Maybe if she had slowed down and allowed herself to think for one second, Will would still be human, and her hand wouldn't be throbbing so hard that she could feel her heartbeat through her skin.

"It's going to be all right," Tom said softly. He put his arm around the back of her chair.

Charlie leaned in close and rested her head on his shoulder.

"I know you're mad at me," she said softly.

"I'm not mad. Frustrated maybe. But not mad," he said.

"That's fair," she said. She shifted in her chair. "I'm sorry. It hurts to lie like that."

"Oh, sweetie. Let me see if I can find out how much longer we'll be." Tom rose from his chair and walked over to the reception desk.

Charlie thumbed through her Favorite contacts. She bypassed Jen who was at the top. As much as she loved her cousin, she wasn't quite ready for Jen to pelt her with questions. She passed Scott's name and Evangeline's and Evan's and finally touched Ben's name. A message popped up, asking her if she wanted to call his number. Yes or No. She took a deep breath and tapped yes. Ben picked up on the first ring.

"Charlie?" It wasn't Ben.

"Hey, Jen," Charlie said. Her voice cracked.

"Well, thank goddess! You have us all going out of our minds here," Jen scolded.

"I'm sorry," Charlie said.

"We're just glad you're alive. I mean, that's what counts."

"So, you're with Ben?"

"Yes, I am. So are Jason and Lisa."

"Hey, Charlie," Jason and Lisa said from what sounded like the back seat.

"Great." Charlie closed her eyes and tried to sound excited. "Hey, Jen, can you take me off speaker and let me talk to Ben for a second, please?"

"Sure," Jen said.

Charlie glanced around. There were too many people

in the waiting room to have this conversation. She hopped to her feet, holding her phone with her left hand against her ear and gasped at the pain in her wrist. She headed for the first exit she saw, avoiding Tom's glance as she walked out the entrance to the patient loading zone in front of the emergency room.

"Hey, Charlie, what's going on?" Ben asked.

"Hang on a second, let me get someplace where I can talk." She walked to the end of the sidewalk away from the automatic doors. "I'm at the ER."

"What happened?" Ben's voice became serious.

Charlie blurted out, "They turned Will." An unexpected onslaught of tears erupted, and for two solid minutes she couldn't get them under control.

"It's okay. It's okay. Just take your time," Ben said.

"Suh-sorry," she mumbled. After a deep breath, she pulled herself together enough to speak again. The words flooded out of her, and she told Ben the whole story. In what felt like one breath. When she was done, she gasped for air.

"I'm just waiting my turn to be seen by a doctor. Broken hand is not as dire as blood loss, so I have to wait."

"And Tom is there with you?"

Charlie turned and saw Tom approaching.

"Yeah, he is."

"Good. I'm glad you're not there alone. We left right

after you called so we're going to be there soon. Maybe another couple of hours."

"No problem," Charlie said. "Is there a cure? For Will I mean?"

"Possibly. I need to make some calls. You hang in there, okay? I'll be there soon."

"Thank you," Charlie said and ended the call.

"What's going on?" Tom asked.

"I just called Ben, that's all. I needed to bring him up to speed." Movement in the parking garage across the street from the emergency room entrance caught Charlie's eye. It was him. He'd followed them. The vampire made eye contact with her, a lurid grin on his unnaturally pale face.

"I will kill you," she mouthed. The vampire threw his head back and laughed. He had heard her, just as she expected.

What?" Tom asked, a confused look on his face.

"Nothing," she said. "I wasn't talking to you. I was —"

"What?" Tom followed her line of sight, but the vampire was gone.

"Just talking to myself."

"Charlie?" Tom said, sounding suspicious.

"I thought I saw the vampire that got away," she said softly.

Tom looked again. "He's gone now. Why don't you

come back inside? The nurse said it would only be a few more minutes."

Charlie nodded and let him lead her away.

* * *

CHARLIE RESTED WITH HER EYES CLOSED. THE PAIN IN HER hand seemed to float somewhere out away from her body. All that was left was the heaviness of the pink fiberglass cast that extended from the middle of her fingers to above her wrist.

One of the ER nurses stopped by the small room she occupied that looked out into the hallway. "How are you feeling, Charlie?"

Charlie opened her eyes, and the room spun a little bit. "Hi. I'm sorry, I don't remember your name. The room is moving."

The nurse laughed. "It's Sarah Beth and that would be the Vicodin, honey. Can you tell me your pain level?"

"Right. Three?" Charlie said.

"That's much better than when you came in," the nurse chirped. "Is there anything I can get you?"

"Can you tell me how my friends are?"

"Who are your friends, honey?"

"Will Tucker and Dan Blankenship. They came in by ambulance though. Ahead of me."

"I can check on it."

"Can you also see where my boyfriend is?" Charlie said. "Tom Sharon. Six feet, dark hair, golden-brown eyes you could swim in. Reaper."

The nurse laughed again.

"I see the drugs have taken effect," Tom said from the doorway. "I'm right here, love."

The nurse turned and looked him up and down. "Here he is. And you're right. Definitely eyes you could swim in." The nurse winked at Tom.

"Hey, babe." Charlie held out her good hand and beckoned him to her side. Tom gave the nurse an uncomfortable smile, stepped inside the room and took Charlie's hand. "I'm so glad you're here," she slurred, drugged-out by now.

"I am definitely here," Tom said. He pulled up a chair and took a seat next to her bed. "They're going to release you soon. We just have to wait for someone from billing to come by."

"Did you give them my insurance card?" Charlie asked.

"I think you have to do that, honey, when they come by."

"All... right," Charlie said, her voice slow and dreamy.

"Well, if there's anything else I can do for you, just give me a holler," the nurse said.

"Sure thing," Charlie said. "Don't forget about my friends. I need to know if Will turned into a vampire."

Tom laughed and glanced nervously at the nurse. "It sounds like she's definitely high on her pain meds."

"Oh, don't worry. I've heard much crazier stuff," the nurse reassured him and left the room.

"Well, I see that the drugs have certainly made you talkative." He smoothed the sheet covering her legs.

"Right. Sorry."

"Don't be sorry. I'm trying to decide if I should take advantage of this or not." Tom gave her a sly glance.

"You don't need to trick me to get me to tell you the truth. I had it all planned out. As soon as my hand stopped hurting." Charlie lifted her cast. "Although I was contemplating waiting until Ben came too."

"Why?" Tom said.

"Because he and my cousins are coming. And it will just be easier to tell you all at the same time. Otherwise, I'll be telling the story over and over and over again."

"I see. So, it's more of an economy thing," Tom teased.

Charlie chuckled and squeezed his hand. "Yeah."

"Good to see you laugh." Tom kissed the back of her hand.

"Okay, dammit. You win. I'll tell you everything." Charlie rolled her eyes and grinned.

"I can wait."

"I heard you were looking for me," a familiar voice said from the doorway.

"Dan!" Charlie said. "You're not dead!"

Dan chuckled and approached Charlie's bed. "You think a bunch of vampires can stop me?"

"Course not. You did two tours in Iraq, right?"

"Yes, I did. How're you doing?"

Charlie held up her cast. "My hand is broken."

"I see. Guess you won't be wielding that wand anytime soon," he said quietly.

"I can shoot with my left hand. Just need some practice," she said. Tom cleared his throat and stood up. "Sorry, Dan, this is my boyfriend, Tom Sharon. Tom, this is Dan Blankenship, the detective working the case with me down here"

The two men nodded and shook hands.

"Nice to meet you." Dan appeared to size Tom up. "You were the one she called for at the warehouse."

"Yes." Tom nodded.

"You never did explain exactly how you just appeared out of thin air," Dan said, his voice light, but his expression wary. Tom pulled his chair beneath him and sat.

Charlie lowered her voice. "Tom's a reaper."

Dan's eyes widened. "No shit. Really? Like the Grim Reaper?"

"Something like that," Tom said.

"Holy shit. The way you plowed through those vampires was impressive. I don't think I properly thanked you for showing up. I'm not sure either of us would've lasted much longer."

"I'm glad I could help," Tom said.

Dan shook his head and shifted his gaze to Charlie. "Girl, you know, yesterday morning, I didn't even know such things existed. You certainly know how to keep a man on his toes."

Tom laughed. "Yes, she does."

"So, how are you?" Charlie pointed to the bandages on his arms.

"I got a bunch of bite wounds. They gave me a rabies shot after I told them I was bitten by bats. I gotta come back and get four more shots over the next two weeks."

"And they believed that?" Charlie asked.

"They seemed to. Course, what else are they gonna believe in their shoes," Dan said.

"True. Sometimes it's easier to believe the lie than to even imagine the truth," Tom chimed in.

"You got that right," Dan said.

"Oh, Dan, I'm so sorry. Are you going to take all the shots?"

Dan shrugged. "I figure it can't hurt. Who knows what the hell those things had in their mouths?"

"True," she said.

"So, how's your friend?"

"I don't know," Charlie said. "I'm hoping they'll tell me something soon."

"Well, I called my wife, and she's coming to pick me

up. They sprung me, so I'm gonna go ahead and head out."

"Okay," Charlie said. "I wouldn't blame you if you don't want to work with me anymore."

"Are you kidding me? This is the best time I've had in I can't remember when." Dan touched her foot and gave it a squeeze. "I think we should both take the next couple days off work, I guess. Maybe regroup on Monday?"

"Yeah, we can do that."

"All right, you take care of her," Dan said to Tom.

"Don't you worry. I'm not going anywhere," Tom said. "And I promise she's in good hands."

Dan gave Tom a nod of approval, turned, and left the room.

"He seems like a good guy," Tom said.

"Yeah, he is," Charlie said. "I'm really glad he didn't die."

"I'm sure he is too."

Charlie's eyes grew heavy. "I'm so tired."

"I know, love," Tom said. "It won't be long. Why don't you rest your eyes? And as soon as all the paperwork gets taken care of, I'll take you back to the hotel."

"What if he's there?" Charlie said. "I swear I saw him outside."

"Don't you worry about the vampire. He will never get near you again," Tom said. Charlie lifted her hand and cupped his cheek.

"You're so good to me. I don't deserve you."

"We're good to each other," Tom said. "Rest now."

"Just for a second. Just until the billing lady comes," Charlie said, the last words feeling mushy in her mouth before she closed her eyes and slept.

CHAPTER 20

Charlie awoke with a scream caught in her throat. She sat up, and the room spun a little bit. She tried to put her face in her hands but bonked herself in the nose with her cast. For a second, a sharp pain shot through her face, and stars bloomed like fireworks before her eyes. The weight of the cast drew her arm down, and she let it rest in her lap.

She closed her eyes, and took several deep breaths to clear the pain, but also to chase away the aftereffects of the dream that had woken her. It still clung to her skin, like the blood of the vampires she'd fought last night. Their shadows moved through her mind, circling her, rushing at her, clawing at her. The memory of the vampire that threw her to the ground like she weighed nothing had imprinted itself on her arms. She lifted the sleeve of her T-shirt and noted the fresh bruises, shaped like a finger. In the dream, it wasn't the vampire she'd encountered last night that was on top of her, grinding her hand into the concrete – it was Will. He was transformed, his formerly handsome face a pallid horrifying mask. His teeth glinted in the light, sharp and deadly ready to drain her of all her blood.

"Charlie? Are you okay?"

Charlie turned her head to face the owner of the unexpected voice next to her in the king-sized bed. "Jen? Where's Tom?"

"He and Ben went to check the perimeter of the building. They're putting a vampire warning spell on the hotel. I think Lisa and Jason are still sleeping."

"In here?" Charlie scanned the room.

"No, honey." Jen chuckled. "They got their own room. Ben and I did, too. But I told him I would sit with you until you woke up. Or they came back. Whichever comes first."

"I can't believe y'all came. I mean, I expected Ben to, but –"

"Did you think we were just going to let you fight off vampires by yourself?"

"No. Of course not." Charlie frowned and rubbed her eyes. Her hand was beginning to throb again. "It's just... this whole trip has been much more dangerous than I anticipated, and I don't want y'all to get hurt, too."

Jen reached across the bed and put her hand on Charlie's shoulder. "Nobody's getting hurt. Okay? You just need to concentrate on resting today. You've been through a lot."

"What's going on with Will?" Charlie asked.

Jen played with the edge of the comforter. "Ben talked to someone at the DOL hospital early this morning, and they're consulting with the doctors here. They're going to put him into a medically induced coma to help slow down his transformation. And he's going to be transported to the DOL hospital for treatment."

"Treatment? There is no treatment, I mean not unless we can catch the sire and take his blood."

"Ew. How is that a treatment?"

"Will told me that if a victim is turned, the whole thing can be reversed as long as he doesn't feed and is injected with the blood of the sire." Charlie pushed the covers back and threw her legs over the side. "When is he leaving? I've got to go the hospital and see him."

"I don't know, honey." Alarm edged into Jen's voice. "I don't think that's a good idea. You need to stay put."

Charlie went to the wide bureau in front of a long mirror hanging on the wall. She avoided looking at her reflection, knowing how haggard and pain-wracked she must look. Instead, she searched through her suitcase and grabbed the first pair of jeans she found. She stuck one foot in first and then the other. They slid comfortably over her narrow hips, but she struggled with the button and zipper because of the way her cast splinted the last three fingers and her hand. She leaned against the bureau, and after a minute of fumbling, she got them closed.

"This is gonna be fun," she grumbled.

"How're you gonna get there?" Jen asked.

"I'll take an Uber." Charlie slipped her bare feet into her tennis shoes. She glanced down and realized she was wearing an oversized Kinks T-shirt that didn't belong to her. "Where did this come from?"

"It's one of Ben's," Jen said. "I couldn't find anything else to put you in last night. And your shirt was so gross and bloody, I suggested we burn it."

"You burned my T-shirt? That was one of my favorites." Charlie tucked the T-shirt into her jeans, pulled a hoodie out of her bag and slid it over her head.

"Of course, I didn't burn it. It's on the soak cycle with some oxygen bleach in the laundry room down the hall."

"Well, thank goddess for that." Charlie glared at her cousin and slipped the strap to her bag over her head, settling it across her body. "Are you just gonna sit there, or are you gonna go with me?"

"I don't think Ben's gonna let you leave."

Charlie put her hands on her hips and cocked her head.

"You don't think he's going to *let* me?" The idea that

anyone would let her do something got her dander up. "We'll just see about that."

Charlie opened the flap of her bag and checked the front pocket for her keycard.

"You looking for this?" Jen asked.

"Give me that." Charlie held her hand out. Jen shook her head.

"Nope. You get back in bed."

"Come on, Jen, I don't need you to mother hen me." Charlie held her hand out. Jen made a face but handed over the card.

"Thank you. Now put your shoes on, please. You're driving me to the hospital."

"What happened to your Uber?" Jen said.

"I changed my mind. Now let's go, please."

* * *

BEN TOOK LESS CONVINCING THAN JEN AND DROVE CHARLIE to the hospital.

"I'm not sure when they're gonna start the transfer, Charlie. I'm not even sure he's still going to be there," Ben said.

"He has to be. I have to talk to him." Charlie stared anxiously out the passenger window of Ben's FJ50. She bounced a little in her seat when he made the turn into the hospital's parking lot. "Can you just drop me off?"

"Sure." Ben drove up to the loading zone in front of the hospital front door. "I'm gonna go park. I'll see you up there."

Charlie nodded and climbed out of the truck. Once inside the airy lobby, she got her bearings and headed for the reception desk.

Charlie put on her best polite smile and approached the woman with a sleek silver bob sitting behind the desk. She looked up from her computer screen and mirrored Charlie's smile.

"Hi. I'm looking for a patient," Charlie said. "William Tucker."

"Okay. Let me just see where he is." The woman's finger crept slowly over the keyboard.

Charlie tapped her foot on the pale gray and white carpeting. She glanced at the clock on the wall behind the desk. "Are you finding him? Or ..."

"Oh, yes, here he is. He's in room 593." The woman wrote the room number on a visitor's pass, and then handed it to Charlie.

"Thank you." Charlie gave her an appreciative smile and clipped the pass to her hoodie. "Where are the elevators, please?"

"Just down that hall, past the stairs to your left." The receptionist pointed to a long hallway across the lobby.

"Thanks," Charlie said and headed that way. A few

minutes later, she poked her head into Will's room and called out, "Knock, knock."

"Charlie?"

She entered the darkened room and found Will sitting up, propped up with pillows. The shades over the one window in the room were pulled down, and most of the lights were off except for the panel behind his bed. On the wall, the darkened screen of the television mirrored the room. Will shifted in his bed as best he could. Charlie tried not to show her shock at his appearance. The transformation had already begun–his skin looked pale and grayish. Dark red circles extended from his bloodshot eyes, and his lips were almost blue. She took a deep breath and forced a smile.

"You're awake," she said.

"Yeah. For now." Will's shoulders sagged.

"Ben said they were gonna put you into a coma. Been there, done that. Got the T-shirt," she teased.

Will chuckled. "You'll have to give me some pointers."

"If you see a light, don't go into it. That's my one tip. Fight it." Charlie moved farther into the room. She spotted a chair in the corner and, with her good hand, dragged it across the floor next to Will's bed. The sight of the restraints on his wrists sobered her mood. Will caught her staring and wiggled his hands.

"Yeah, these are for my own protection. Something about seizures. I think that's what the docs from the DOL told them here." He shrugged. "It's fine. It won't matter in a little while anyway."

Charlie took a seat and put her good hand on top of his. Will's gaze shifted to her cast.

"I'm sorry about your wrist."

"It's just a fracture. It'll heal."

"I'm glad to see you're still alive."

"Ditto." She squeezed his hand tighter.

Will laughed but made a bitter face. "Yeah, I'm only half dead. And who knows if this whole coma thing's gonna work or not."

"It will work. We're gonna find the sire. You can't give up on me, you hear me? That is not allowed."

Will nodded but averted his eyes and stared into the shadows of the room.

"You know, when you get better, you and I need to have a long talk about this need of yours to hunt vampires at any cost."

"If I get better."

"Will, you have to fight."

"Maybe it's better if the DOL just kills me now." Will finally met her eyes.

"Is that what you wanted? To just die by a vampire attack? Is that why..." Charlie softened her tone.

Will's jaw tightened, and his fingers stretched out beneath the weight of hers. Charlie pulled her hand away. She leaned forward in her chair and rested her elbows on her knees. The tile floor of the room looked dingy gray in the dim light.

"About a year before I left my husband, I thought the world would be better off without me. I thought my *son* would be better off without me."

"I know what you're saying, but..." Will started. "I don't have anyone to leave behind."

Charlie straightened up in her chair. "Now, you listen to me Will Tucker. You are not alone in this world. Not anymore. You are my partner and my friend, and I need you."

Will's expression morphed to shock, and his eyes glinted with wetness. "The last person who needed me ended up dead."

"Your old partner," Charlie said softly. Charlie had sensed something about the woman's death when she first met Will, but he'd been evasive and light on the details whenever she asked about her before.

"Actually, she was my wife. I tell people she was my partner because they might feel sympathy, but they don't pity me. When you tell people it's your wife who died, they straight up pity you, and I can't bear that. Especially since it was my fault she died."

"Oh, Will, I'm so sorry."

"See, there it is."

"No. This isn't pity. This is sorrow. Sorrow for someone I care about."

Will sniffled and his head fell back against the pillow. "My wife would've liked you. She could be sensitive too."

"How long has she been gone again?"

"Twelve months and sixteen days," he said.

Charlie reached for him again, laying her hand over his. This grief still stabbed at him every day. Every damned day, and she hadn't noticed. Had been so wrapped up in the loss of her abilities. Guilt flooded her heart, and she hung her head.

"I'm sorry," she said. "I should've seen you were suffering."

"I want you to promise me something." Will took a deep breath.

"Sure. Anything."

"I don't want to finish the transformation. If you cannot find the sire, I need you to kill me."

"What? No! No. No." She shook her head. "You are going to be fine. We're going to find him, and you are not going to transform, do you hear me?"

"Promise me, Charlie. Promise me that you will make sure that I never drink from a human being ever. Promise me that you will kill me."

Charlie gritted her teeth. "I will make sure you never drink from a human being."

"Please? Please, Charlie. It won't be me anymore."

"It's not gonna come to that, but if it does, I will make

sure that the DOL puts you down as humanely as possible."

"I'll take that. Thank you. There's one other thing."

"What?" Charlie asked warily.

"If I do turn, or if y'all have to kill me, I want you to have my car."

Charlie laughed and some of the tension eased out of the room. "Will, that's very sweet, but isn't there somebody else you'd rather leave it to?"

"No. There is only one person, and I haven't seen him in like ten years, so it's yours."

"Tell me his name, and Athena will find him."

"You don't want my car?" Will sounded a little offended.

"I didn't say that. I just—"

"I'm just kidding. But seriously, I want you to have it. I trust you. You'll take care of it."

A knock at the door drew their attention. A short nurse in pink scrubs with her hair pulled back into a messy bun appeared. "I'm sorry to break this up, but Will's transport is here. It's time."

"Thanks." Will flipped his hand up and caught hold of Charlie's fingers. He gave them a tight squeeze. "You take care of yourself."

"I'll see you soon."

"Sure." Will nodded. He released her hand and

Charlie stood up. "Hey, if you do manage to capture that son of a bitch," he said. "make it hurt for me. Okay?"

"That's one promise I don't mind making," Charlie said. "I'll see you later."

The nurse shooed her out into the hall, and Charlie couldn't help but feel this might be the last time she would ever see Will Tucker alive.

CHAPTER 21

Charlie stared through the windshield of Ben's truck at the bank of billowing gray clouds gathering in the distance. With her free hand, she held the tail of the seatbelt pulled tight across her lap. Her knuckles kept scraping against the rough fiberglass wrap of her cast. She fidgeted, not quite shaking the last image of Will in his bed or the hopelessness in his voice.

Charlie broke the comfortable silence in the truck. "What happens to Will if we can't catch the son of a bitch?"

"I don't know," Ben said. He turned on his blinker and looked over his shoulder before he changed lanes. "But we're gonna do everything we can to find this vampire. Okay? Not just for Will but for you, too. From what you described he's obviously obsessed with you. And vampire obsession is nothing to screw around with."

"Hmm. Will told me the same thing once. He said the only thing worse was reaper obsession. Looks like I've just broken all the rules, haven't I?"

"Tom's a good guy. And I've never seen him act that way toward you."

"Neither have I. Makes me wonder where Will got his information." Charlie noticed a sign for Johnny's Pancake House a few hundred yards before Ben took the highway exit. Her stomach growled a little. It had been over twenty-four hours since she and Dan had gotten lunch together.

Ben looked over at her before shifting his eyes back to the road. "You know, tomorrow if you're feeling up to it, maybe you and Jason and I can go question the High Priestess. She's still on your list to be interviewed, right?"

"Yes, she is. I should probably text her because I had planned to meet with her today."

"Good. I'd like to wrap this case up as soon as we can.
"

"Me, too. And just for the record, I'm up to it now. I mean, my hand hurts, but I've certainly dealt with worse."

"You know, I could try to heal it," Ben said.

Charlie shifted in her seat. "I appreciate that, but I think it's better if I just let it heal the old-fashioned way.

It's not that I don't trust your abilities or anything like that..."

"Of course not." Ben gave her a sly smile.

"I just don't feel like messing with taking this cast off. Right now, that might hurt worse than anything else."

"Okay. If you change your mind..."

"I will let you know."

"When we get back to the hotel, let's go over some strategy for taking another pass at the mother and boyfriend."

"Sure."

"Of course, we'll defer to whatever you sensed from them yesterday, but I don't like that they lied."

"Me, either." Charlie cleared her throat and sank down into her seat. "You know, when we get back to the hotel room, there's something I need to tell y'all."

Ben slowed down and took the exit for the hotel. "Are you okay?"

"Yeah, I'm fine. Fine." Charlie nodded. "Really. Just fine."

"That's an awful lot of fines." Ben smirked at her.

Charlie sighed. "Can I ask you a question?"

"Of course."

"What sort of things would get me fired?"

"What?" Ben snorted. "What on the goddess's green earth would make you ask that? You do know you're doing a great job, right? Have I not told you that?"

"You have. And I appreciate that. But I still need to know."

"Okay." Ben cleared his throat and twisted his head, working out a crick in his neck. "It actually takes a lot to get fired from the DOL. It's a lot like working for the government." Ben cut his eyes toward her. "What's this all about?"

Charlie pressed her head against the headrest and grimaced. She closed her eyes and blurted out, "I'm not psychic anymore." The words hung in the air between them. Her skin twitched, waiting for Ben's reaction. She slanted a look at him.

Ben pressed his lips together and grew quiet.

"Are you mad?"

"Mad that you're not psychic anymore? No, of course not." He gave her a reassuring glance. "I just...I should have figured it out. I knew something was going on with you."

"Nobody knew. I haven't even said it out loud before now."

"You are a very good actress."

"I never acted. I always answered you honestly. You just never asked me outright..." Ben gave her a pointed look. Charlie squirmed in her seat.

Ben's hands tightened around his steering wheel, and his knuckles whitened. "You're right. I didn't."

"You sure you're not mad?"

"I'm not mad. I promise. I'm amazed. You've done a great job with your cases so far, even without your psychic abilities. Which speaks to your strengths as a witch. I'm surprised you haven't compensated more with magic."

"What do you mean?" Charlie asked.

"There are plenty of witches who aren't psychic, Charlie. But it doesn't mean they don't use tools to help them read a situation or even read a mind or two. You obviously had an encounter with Ariel's spirit, which means you're not completely blind to the spirit world."

"I know." Charlie poked her bottom lip out a little. "But I can't see them."

"You don't have to see them to deal with them. You've proven that."

"It's just so much easier when I can see them."

"Yeah, but, even in the past, you've dealt with spirits that aren't forthcoming with the information you want."

"That's true. Ariel has been much more honest than some of the spirits I have encountered before. Maybe because our communication is so limited."

"Maybe so. See, there's a silver lining."

"I wouldn't go that far."

"Tell me something. If you had the chance to get your abilities back, would you? It's caused a lot of grief in the past."

"I have thought about this. A lot. And the answer to that question is yes. I feel like a piece of me is missing."

"Have you told anybody else?"

"No. I haven't even told Tom. And it has frustrated the hell out of him. Trust me."

"I imagine it has. I'm really glad you told me, though. I appreciate your trust."

"You have no idea how hard it is to fake being psychic around a bunch of witches who have very sharp intuition."

"Just keep in mind that your intuition is just as sharp as theirs. And that is something that no one can take from you."

"Thank you."

"So, when did this happen?"

"After I died," Charlie said softly.

"Hmmm. What's your plan? Are you gonna tell everyone?"

"Yeah, I think so. I pretty much promised Tom I would tell them everything that was going on."

"Good. I think that's the right move. Maybe we can put our heads together and figure out exactly what happened and if there's a way to help you."

"I would appreciate that. I hadn't really thought there could be a way to restore my abilities."

"Well, we should see what we can do. What's the worst thing that could happen?"

"I stay like this forever?" Charlie said.

"Exactly." Ben turned into the parking lot of the hotel. "Of course, I don't envy you."

"Why is that?"

"I certainly wouldn't want to be the one to tell your cousins that you've been keeping a secret from them."

"Oh, they know. Or at least, they know something's up, and it's probably driving them nuts that they haven't figured it out yet." Charlie laughed. "Don't worry about my cousins. I can handle them."

"Oh, really? Then why haven't you told them before today?" Ben teased and turned into a parking space near the back entrance of the hotel.

Charlie's mouth gaped, and her brow furrowed. "Oh, hush."

Ben laughed and put the car in park.

"I CAN'T BELIEVE YOU DIDN'T TELL US." JEN CROSSED HER arms and glared at Charlie, a hurt expression on her heart-shaped face. Charlie scanned the faces of her family and friends sitting throughout her hotel room. Their eyes all trained on her.

Lisa grinned and snapped her fingers at Jason. "Pay up."

Jason protested. "No. You didn't get it exactly right."

"I got closer than you did." Lisa waggled her fingers.

"You guys placed a bet on whether I was still psychic?" Charlie put her good hand on her hip.

"It was Jason's idea." Lisa held her hands up defensively.

Jason made an indignant noise in the back of his throat. "I should have known you'd throw me under the bus. What I said was that you seemed to be avoiding me and Lisa is the one that said your energy was off."

"Yes, I did, and I was right, so you have to pay," said Lisa.

"Fine," Jason grumbled and pulled his wallet out of his back pocket. He slipped a twenty-dollar bill from inside and handed it over to Lisa.

"So, that's what's been going on?" Tom said, sounding relieved. He shook his head and held out his arms and enveloped Charlie in a hug. "I'm sorry you didn't feel like you could tell me." He squeezed her tight. "But I am so happy that you've told us now. It makes so much sense."

"No, it doesn't," Jen said, pouting. "Why didn't you tell us? We could've helped you."

"Jen, come on. We should cut her some slack," Lisa said.

"Says the woman with my twenty-dollar bill," Jason said.

Jen made a frustrated face and rolled her eyes. "Fine. You're forgiven. I'm sorry you've been going through this all by yourself, but we might've been able to help if you had shared."

"Passive-aggressive much?" Lisa said. "Forgiveness doesn't include guilt as a consolation prize."

"Oh, hush, Lisa." Jen stuck her tongue out at her sister.

"Please y'all, don't bicker on my account. I wish I had felt I could share it earlier, and I'm sorry I didn't. Okay?" Charlie said, and withdrew from Tom's arms.

"Okay. I'm sorry too." Jen walked across the room and threw her arms around Charlie, hugging her tight. "When did this happen?"

Charlie gave Jen a squeeze and pulled out of her arms. "After I died."

"Maybe the process of dying closed your third eye," Lisa said.

"Her third eye?" Jason turned and seemed to study Charlie's face.

"Her second sight," Lisa explained and touched the center of her forehead.

"Oh, right." Jason nodded. "Is there a way to open it again?"

"Maybe, assuming Charlie wants to open it again," Lisa said. "It's kind of a heavy burden to be able to feel what others feel and deal with spirits all the time. She might like the peace and quiet."

"That is true," Jen said. "No one would blame you if you didn't want to reopen it."

"It's such a big part of who I am. I've kind of been lost without it," Charlie admitted. Jen looped her arm in Charlie's and gave her a squeeze. "I actually miss it."

Ben leaned against the wall next to the closet, his arms folded across his chest, an intense expression of scrutiny on his face. "I'm just gonna throw this out there. I think you could compensate with magic. There are a lot of spells that let you talk to the dead, let you see the future, even let you hear other's thoughts. It might be worth exploring."

Tom slipped his arm around Charlie's shoulders. "The important thing is that we know what's going on. And nothing has to be done right this minute about it. You're not suffering, are you?"

"Suffering? No of course not. Would it be helpful? Yes, but not being able to sense how irritated Jason is about losing a bet to his girlfriend or how smug she feels is not painful. At all."

"Hey!" Lisa and Jason said in unison.

"What? I still have my intuition." Charlie gave Ben an appreciative glance.

"Yes, you do," Ben said.

Tom kissed her temple. "We just want you to be happy and not in pain."

"Agreed," Jen said.

"Agreed," Lisa said.

"Agreed," Ben said.

"Great, now that we all agree can we go get some lunch or something?" Jason rubbed his belly. "I don't know about y'all, but I am starving. Ben wouldn't even slow down for us to go to the bathroom last night."

A chorus of laughter filled the room, and even Ben joined in.

"I think that's a great idea," Charlie said. "I saw a pancake house near the highway. Who's up for breakfast?"

Everyone in the room raised their hand.

CHAPTER 22

Charlie took one of the long pillows on the king-sized bed and propped up her arm. She preferred sleeping on her right side, but the heaviness of the cast made the pain in her arm impossible. She thought about popping one of the Vicodin that they'd prescribed for her at the hospital, but she hated feeling loopy and out of control.

Tom kept to a schedule of prowling the hotel and grounds for any sign of the vampire. He would pop into the room and check on her now and again. She knew he was only a thought away if she needed him.

The pillow beneath her head kept going lumpy. She adjusted it for what felt like the hundredth time, took a deep breath, and blew it out slowly. The weight of sleep crept into her limbs first, then her eyelids, and she slipped into that place between waking and dreaming.

At first she thought the sound of water was inside her head. Some dream of waterfalls and rain beckoning to her. But the sound grew louder, steadier. She opened her eyes.

"Tom? Is that you?"

No answer. She listened to the sounds of the room. Water gushing somewhere nearby.

Her heart sped up. There was no way the vampire could get into this room. Ben had cast a spell on the lock. Part of her wished that she had taken Jen up on her offer to sleep over, like they were teenagers again.

"Who's there?"

No answer.

This is stupid, Charlie. Get up and look!

Charlie reached for the base of the heavy lamp on the nightstand and pressed the on switch. She quickly scanned the room. Nothing seemed out of order except for the sound of running water. She pushed the covers off and threw her legs over the side of the bed, grabbed her wand off the nightstand with her left hand, and began to investigate.

Thick, billowing steam spilled into the room from the bathroom, making the air sticky and humid. Charlie reached in with her splinted hand, flipped the light switch on the wall, and jerked her arm back. Nothing but the clean, empty bathroom stared back at her.

She stepped inside. Hot water gushed from the spigot into the sink, and steam fogged the large mirror.

"What the hell?" She frowned and turned off the silver handle marked H. Maybe Tom had left it on before he went out to check the perimeter again, and she'd just been too sleepy to notice. She flipped off the bathroom light and went back to bed.

It took her several minutes to find a comfortable position again, but eventually her body relaxed, and her eyelids grew heavy. When she was almost asleep, the sound of water filled her senses again.

"Dammit," she said. She rose from her bed, marched into the bathroom and turned off the spigot again. She stared at it for a moment, daring it to turn on again.

"This is ridiculous," she muttered and turned to leave. The spigot turned itself on again before she could make it out the door.

Charlie reached for the metal handle. The word STOP appeared on the mirror, written by some invisible finger. She stepped backward. The towel rack jammed into her shoulder blade, jarring her arm. A fresh wave of pain made her suck her breath in through her teeth. She cradled her arm for a second until the pain subsided a bit. Her eyes focused on the word etched into the steamy mirror.

"Ariel? Is that you?"

Charlie waited for a sign. Any sign that Ariel had followed her to the hotel and was now trying to communicate with her.

One letter at a time formed on the mirror. When it was finished, Charlie stared at the word. Her good hand drifted to her throat.

WITCHFINDER

"Who is this?" Charlie demanded. "Ariel? This isn't funny." The hot water spigot turned off on its own, and the steam drifted up to the ceiling, floating like a cloud.

In the other room, Charlie heard her phone chirp, signaling a new text. She flipped off the light and marched back to the bed. She glared at her phone on the nightstand, plugged into the USB port on the base of the lamp and charging. She picked it up, swiped up with her thumb, and opened her message app.

A text from Dan Blankenship had just arrived. She tapped the text open and read it under the arc of the lamp.

Text me when you get this. Looks like we're working tomorrow after all.

Charlie had to put the phone on the nightstand to tap out her text with her good hand.

What's going on?

Sorry I woke you.

You didn't. What's happened?

Chase Andrews found dead tonight in his car outside Ariel's old workplace. I have to view security footage of parking lot.

How did he die?

Same as Ariel. Poison. Rash round mouth. Some defensive wounds on hands. Hoping he scratched the SOB. Would love to find some DNA.

DNA would be awesome.

How R U feeling?

Hand hurts, but ok. Have to get my boyfriend or boss to drive me to meet you.

Wrapping up crime scene now.

Ok.

Meet me at Chase Andrews's house in the morning? Say 8:00 a.m.? We can go through it together.

Sounds good. C U then.

CHARLIE STARED AT HER PHONE FOR A MINUTE, AND THEN her eyes drifted to the book that Ariel had thrown at her. The Witches of Europe. She picked it up, thumbed through it and found a folded piece of notebook paper marking a chapter. Charlie unfolded the paper and looked over the note written in a neat feminine script.

Witchfinders were particular to England from 1645 – 1647. Why is Matthew Goodman calling himself a witchfinder? Is that even his real name? It sounds made up. I wish he would just leave me alone. I need to find a spell to banish him. Need some of his hair though and don't want to get that close. Maybe the letters will work. I'm so tired of dealing with this whole situation.

Charlie folded the piece of paper and put it back into the book. She picked up her phone again and as quickly as her fingers would allow, she jotted off a text to Dan.

Just found a note in book I took from Ariel's room. Mentions a Matthew Goodman. Can you run the name and see what comes up?

Sure thing.

Charlie climbed under the covers and turned off the light. She stretched out on her back, easing her casted hand onto her stomach, turning Matthew Goodman's name over in her head until sleep reached up and dragged her into the darkness.

CHAPTER 23

Charlie ran a brush through her hair and quickly twisted the tangled mop into a messy bun at the base of her skull. She finger-combed her bangs and ignored the dark circles beneath her eyes and sallowness of her skin. Maybe when she got home, she would visit her cousin Daphne at her salon. Freshen up her cut and get a facial. Daphne had just put in two massaging and pedicure chairs and hired a manicurist. When all this was said and done, she would treat herself to a little self-care. It would have to do for now. She tucked the pale pink T-shirt into her jeans and turned out the light.

Charlie left the bathroom, and something white on the floor caught her attention. She bent down and picked up the envelope. When had this arrived? She hadn't noticed it last night when she was dealing with the spirit leaving messages on the bathroom mirror. Her name was scrawled on the front but spelled incorrectly.

Charlie Paine

She shook her head and jammed her thumb underneath the flap. The ripping sound of the paper was oddly satisfying. Inside she found a single piece of thin cheap copier paper folded in thirds.

CHARLIE PAINE,

Stop meddling where you don't belong and I won't kill you right away. Continue and you'll have the same fate as your father and aunt.

SINCERELY,

Matthew Goodman, Witchfinder

"YEAH, TAKE A NUMBER, BUDDY," SHE MUTTERED AND rolled her eyes. She didn't know whether to laugh or be terrified by the threat.

Her eyes scanned the second line again and her stomach fluttered. Was this idiot really claiming that he was somehow involved in the deaths of her parents and aunt? As far as she knew, her parents had died in a car accident after her father had fallen asleep at the wheel. Her Aunt Ellen, Jen and Lisa's mother, and Uncle Jack's wife had died from a severe asthma attack. She folded the letter and put it into the envelope, taking care not to get her fingerprints all over it. She put it on the edge of the bed and quickly unplugged her phone. Her fingers fumbled, and the phone dropped onto the carpet.

"Dammit."

A knock on her door startled her. She scooped up her phone with her left hand and went to the door. "Who is it?"

"It's Ben."

Charlie pushed the metal latch away and turned the deadbolt.

"Hey," she said, a little breathless. Ben and Jason greeted her with concern etched on their faces. She stepped back, opening the door wide. "Come on in."

"What's wrong?" Ben asked.

"Nothing's wrong exactly." She scratched her forehead. "Jason, you wouldn't happen to have any evidence bags with you, would you?"

"I'm not sure," Jason said. "What's going on?"

"I don't have any gloves with me, either, and I don't want y'all to touch it."

"Touch what?" Ben asked.

"I got a letter under my door. I need to take it to Dan

so that he can have it fingerprinted and checked for any sort of biological material."

"Who was the letter from?" Jason asked.

"Come on. I'll show you." Charlie waved them inside. "It's from the guy calling himself the witchfinder."

Jason and Ben exchanged glances. Charlie closed the door behind them, and they followed her into the room. Charlie ducked into the bathroom and grabbed a couple of pieces of tissue from the holder on the counter. When she joined them, she used the tissue to keep her prints from contaminating the envelope and letter more than they already had. She unfolded the letter and laid it out on the bed.

Jason knelt and read the letter. "He's not very bright, is he?"

"It could be an alias," Ben said.

"Yeah, it probably is, but my guess is this isn't his first rodeo. He's confident, cocky even. He wants her to know who he is and to fear him. I bet he even thinks he's smart enough to get away with it."

Ben rubbed the back of his neck, a serious scowl on his face. He sighed. "You're probably right, which means there are more victims out there that we haven't tied together. Charlie, what do you know about your parents' and your aunt's deaths?"

"My parents died in a car accident, and my aunt died

from an asthma attack. Jen or Uncle Jack could tell you more."

"I'm gonna give Athena a call. Get her searching the databases."

"Tell her I'm sorry. Hopefully, once we solve this, she'll actually get a whole weekend off," Charlie said. "I'm gonna give Dan a call and let him know. Since it's his case, too."

"Sure." Ben pulled his phone from his messenger bag and stepped out into the hallway to make his call.

Jason jerked his thumb toward the door. "I'll go see if I've got an evidence bag that we can put that in."

"Thank you." Charlie patted him on the arm, and once he was gone, texted Dan with the situation. Her phone vibrated in her hand

"Hey, Dan," Charlie said.

"Are you kidding me?" Dan asked. "He wrote you a letter?"

"No joke. Dead serious. Jason's gonna see if he has some baggies so we can at least keep it clean till I can hand it off to you. I've touched it, though, so you'll need to take my fingerprints," Charlie said.

"No problem. We've got a new fingerprint scanner that makes it very easy," Dan said.

"That's very cool," Charlie said

"Yeah, we like it. So, when did you get this note?"

"Sometime between the time that you texted last

night about Chase and this morning when I was getting dressed in the bathroom. I didn't notice it until I was getting ready to leave."

"That's about a four-hour difference. Wonder if the hotel has security in the halls."

"I can check on that."

"Listen, I'm gonna swing by the hotel, talk to the manager about getting any security footage. Maybe even if there's nothing in the halls, they at least have cameras in the parking lot."

"Sure. Let's just hope he didn't think about parking where we couldn't see him," Charlie said.

"This guy is signing his name to his letters. Not sure he's the sharpest tool in the shed if you know what I mean."

"Jason said that this Goodman guy sounds cocky and may not think he's gonna get caught."

"This Jason guy sounds like he's seen a thing or two."

"Yeah, he has." Charlie smiled, flashing on working with Jason. "He's my old partner at the Sheriff's department in my home county."

"We can all put our heads together on this one. Hopefully, we'll get lucky, and we'll find some fingerprints on that letter. I've got a forensic team headed over to Chase Andrews's house this morning. Maybe he got sloppy when he took Chase."

"We can hope."

"All right, stay put. And please don't go anywhere by yourself. Even though you sound calm about it, it's still a threat we should take seriously considering," Dan said.

"Oh don't worry about me. I've got a reaper for a guard dog and he's the last thing this Goodman is gonna want to mess with."

"Good. See you soon."

"I'll be here," Charlie said.

DAN ARRIVED AT CHARLIE'S ROOM, AND SHE MADE ALL THE introductions. It amazed her how easily he accepted not only her and Ben but also the rest of her crew, including her cousins. Jason had found an extra evidence bag and a pair of gloves at the bottom of his duffel bag. He'd put the letter inside for safekeeping.

Charlie, Ben, and Jason watched as Dan read the letter through the clear evidence bag. "I've already put in a request to pull a full background check for Matthew Goodman. With any luck, this guy's in our system. Although, I probably won't have any information about DNA or preliminary cause of death for at least a month," Dan said.

"The wheels do turn slow sometimes," Jason added.

Dan nodded with a look of regret. "Yep."

"Maybe I can help with that," Ben offered. "It would take some cooperation on your medical examiner's part."

"Yeah, I appreciate that. But I don't want to get the waters all muddy. I mean, this guy doesn't look like he's an actual witch. So—"

"I understand, and I agree. If this guy is just your run of the mill murderer, he's better off in your justice system than ours," Ben said. "But we're happy to help speed things up as long as it doesn't interfere with your investigation."

"Thanks. I'll think about it," Dan said.

"What did the manager say about the security footage?" Jason asked. "I noticed cameras in the hall and the parking lot."

"He's getting it for me now."

"If you need an extra pair of hands or eyes, I'm happy to help." Jason chuckled. " Seems like I spend a lot of time these days looking through videos of parking lots."

"I hear you on that," Dan said. "If you don't mind, I'll take all the help I can get on this."

"I don't mind."

"Great. I'll set you up at my station house with a monitor."

"That'd be great," Jason said.

"What do you need me to do?" Charlie tried to fold her arms across her chest but found it awkward with her cast. She dropped her free hand to her side and kept her cast elevated. "I feel like I need to do something."

"I still need to look at Chase's house. You could help me with that. You could too, Ben, if you want to," Dan said.

"Let's do it," Ben said.

"All right. I'll get a deputy to take you over to the Sheriff's station, Jason. He'll set you up so you can start watching the security footage."

"Cool. I'm just gonna run and tell Lisa what's going on. She's getting a little antsy." Jason left the room.

"You know you're gonna have to bring Tom," Ben said. "I'm surprised he's not in here hovering."

"He's just a little protective. And honestly, I'm not unhappy about it at the moment, considering I now have a vampire and a witchfinder gunning for me." Charlie shrugged. "Plus, he can surveil things in a way none of us can."

"What do you mean?" Dan asked.

"In his natural reaper form, he's invisible. He only shows that form if he wants to be seen. It can be pretty terrifying staring at a reaper in full robes with a scythe in this hand," Ben explained.

"Which is why he wears a glamour when he's with us." Charlie ticked her head from side to side. "Most of the time."

Dan laughed, his thick neck reddening. "Y'all, I know

I should be losing my mind over all this stuff that y'all keep throwing at me. But it's the most fascinating thing I've encountered in I can't remember when." He shook his head. "It's crazy to think there's this whole other world existing side-by-side with me and my run-of-the-mill murderers."

"I, for one, am glad you're not losing your mind. Your acceptance has been so nice." Charlie patted Dan on the upper arm. He winced and sucked in his breath through his teeth. "Oh, Dan, I'm so sorry. I forgot about your bites."

"It's all right." Dan rubbed the side of his arm. "Y'all ready to get out of here?"

"Absolutely," Charlie crowed, happy not to be cooped up in her room anymore.

CHAPTER 24

The vampire wore his sunglasses into the beach shop. He milled about the racks of T-shirts, bathing suits, and beach wraps, biding his time. He'd seen the old woman who owned the shop leave half an hour ago, cross the street, and order lunch from the sandwich shop.

He set himself close to the door, pretending to peruse a rack of cheap sunglasses, the better to watch her through the glass storefront. The witch left the sandwich shop with two large bags in hand. She moved slowly, her generous body and wide hips hidden under a bright purple Hawaiian muumuu with yellow hibiscus flowers rippling with every step. Her wiry salt and pepper hair reached her shoulders, and she wore thick-framed sunglasses that hid her eyes and half of her face.

The bell jingled overhead when she passed through the doors, and the vampire could hear her heavy breathing from the exertion of crossing the street. The sound almost drowned out the fast beat of her heart. He tried not to imagine the muscle in her chest pumping the blood through her ample body. He was well fed. What he needed was a spell.

He followed her to the back of the store, where a pimply-faced clerk sat behind the register. He jumped to attention when he saw his boss approaching and raised the pass-through so she could come behind the register. Her wide hips brushed the sides of the counter.

"Here you go, Sean." The witch handed the clerk one of the bags. He gladly took it and dove into its contents, leaving the flip-up raised. The witch disappeared into the back office, and the vampire waltzed past the clerk and headed into the office behind the witch.

"Hey! You can't be back there," Sean protested. He put his lunch down next to the register and followed the vampire.

The witch stood in front of her desk. Her dark-brown eyes were trained on the vampire. From her wary expression and the wrinkling of her nose, she knew exactly what he was. Good. There would be no explanation necessary.

"I'm sorry, Myra, this guy just pushed his way back here. Do you want me to throw him out?"

"Yes, Myra," the vampire purred. "Do you want him to throw me out?"

Myra kept one eye on him and smiled at Sean. "It's fine. You eat your lunch. This won't take long. Will it, Mr.?"

"Roman Leander at your service," the vampire said.

Sean glanced from Myra to the vampire and back to his boss again. "You sure?"

"Yeah. Go on now. And close the door, please," Myra said. Sean kept his gaze on Roman until the door was completely shut behind him. "So... to what do I owe this honor?" Myra pulled out her oversized office chair and sat down with a grunt.

"I need a spell."

"Do you?" Myra looked him up and down, sizing him up. She leaned forward over her desk and put her hand on a hilt of a silver letter opener shaped like a dagger she kept near her crystal ball. "What kind of spell?"

"There's a reaper that's getting in my way, and I need him gone."

Myra's eyes widened and her jowls shook a little when her lips curved down. "Interesting. And what makes you think I can do such a spell."

"A friend told me you specialize in the dark arts, and that you could possibly facilitate such a thing."

"Messing with Death's reapers is a dangerous business, if you know what I mean."

"I have no soul, Myra, so have no use for reapers."

"And yet you want to banish one." She eyed him with curiosity. "What has this reaper ever done to you?"

"He's protecting a human I want. A witch. She and her partner murdered my entire nest. My progeny. She can't be allowed to live."

"Interesting. I can do it, but it won't last long. A half hour at best. They're eternal creatures after all." She tipped her head.

"I only need him gone long enough to kill her and her family," Roman said flatly.

"Fine. I'll need some special ingredients. It may take me a few days to get them, and it's going to cost you. Cash. No gold or silver or whatever coinage you've collected over the decades of your life. Good old American currency."

"Name your price, witch," Roman said.

"A thousand dollars," the witch said. "Like I said. Cash."

"You have a deal." He extended his hand to shake.

"Sorry, I don't touch other creatures."

Roman chuckled and lowered his hand. "You are a smart witch. I'll be back on Friday. I assume that will be ample time."

"You'll have your spell then," Myra said.

Roman opened the door. "It's good doing business with you."

Myra smiled. "Close the door on your way out."

Roman gave her a little salute and left her to her sandwich.

"See you Friday, Sean," Roman said as he passed through the flip-up again. Then he sauntered out of the shop.

CHAPTER 25

Dan parked the Tahoe in front of Chase Andrews's house. No glamour covered the tidy little bungalow today. It looked almost exactly as it did after Charlie broke the illusion that had been hiding Chase in plain sight.

The team of four exited the truck.

"I'll make a sweep around the house," Tom said. He reached for Charlie's good arm and gave it a gentle squeeze, speaking low in her ear, "I'll be nearby if you need me. You know what to do."

"Thank you, sweetie," she said. From the corner of her eye, she saw Dan watching them. His face filled with wonder when Tom dropped his glamour for a split second, then disappeared as if into thin air. Charlie chuckled to herself. She resisted telling Dan to close his mouth because he was drawing flies.

She turned her attention back to the others. "Y'all already?" she asked.

"Yep." Dan handed Ben and Charlie pairs of gloves and booties to cover their shoes. Then he led the way through the gate and up the walkway to the front door. Once they were on the front porch, they all slipped the booties over their shoes and donned the gloves. Dan gave the door handle a twist, and it resisted.

"Here, let me." Ben slipped his hand out of the glove and held it over the nickel doorknob but didn't touch it. The lock clicked, and Ben made quick work of unlocking the deadbolt as well. He slipped his hand back into the glove, turned the knob, and pushed the door open.

"Ladies first," Ben said.

Charlie nodded her thank you and stepped into the foyer, her wand up, ready for whatever came next. Dan followed closely behind, but Ben stayed on the porch a few minutes longer. Charlie glanced around the foyer into the tidy living room. It looked untouched. When she realized Ben was still outside, she popped her head out the door. "Everything okay?"

"Yeah. Everything's fine," he said, but nothing in his voice or stance convinced her he meant it.

"What is it?" she asked.

"I can't explain it, but I feel like we're being watched,"

Ben said, his gaze moving from one end of the street to the other. "And the worst part is I don't know if it's this witchfinder guy or the vampire."

Charlie's stomach dropped like a cold icy rock, and she pressed her hand to her belly. "I know what you mean. I can feel it too." She shrugged. "Either way, there's nothing we can do from out here. Tom's keeping watch."

"Yeah." Ben nodded.

"I wish I could do more than just feel like there might be someone out there," she confessed. "Three months ago, I could've told you for sure."

"Hey. Don't worry about that right now. Jen has some ideas worth exploring about getting that fixed."

Charlie's shoulders slumped, despite Ben's optimistic news. "Once we're done with this case, I'm open to trying."

"We should probably get inside before one of the neighbors gets too nosy."

Charlie agreed, and they entered the house, closing the door tightly behind them.

"Dan?" Charlie called.

"In the kitchen," he answered. They found Dan bent over a glass lying on its side on the floor.

"What have you got?" Charlie asked.

"Not sure." Dan took a stack of numbered plastic markers and dropped one next to the glass.

Ben walked across the kitchen. "Look at this." He

gestured to a mortar and pestle shoved into a half-open drawer. He pulled the black granite bowl out of the drawer and put it on the counter. "Whoever used this last did a crappy job of cleaning it."

Charlie and Dan both peered into the bowl. Little bits of a green substance stuck to the inside of the porous surface. Dan dropped another marker next to the mortar and pestle. "You found it in there?" Dan pointed to the drawer.

"Yeah," Ben said.

Dan dropped another marker. "My forensics team should be here soon. They can print and collect all this evidence."

"Great," Ben said.

Charlie moved out of the kitchen into a small dining room. "Hey, y'all? Can y'all come in here and look at this?"

"Well, I think we found the crime scene," Dan said when he came in behind Ben.

One of the two chairs knocked sideways on the floor had a broken brace, as if it had been snapped out by force. The brace itself was nowhere to be seen. Blood spatter dotted the clean vanilla-colored walls.

"Was Chase stabbed at all?" Charlie knelt next to the broken chair.

"No, he wasn't," Dan said. "His arms and hands were

bruised up, and it looked like he had something underneath his nails. But he didn't have any other wounds."

"So what caused this?" Ben asked. He pointed to the spatter on the wall.

"Chase must've hurt our good friend the witchfinder," Dan said. He dropped markers on the floor in front of the wall and next to each of the chairs.

"Physical evidence is great," Charlie said. "If he's hurt, maybe he went to a hospital."

"Maybe," Dan said. "Certainly something we can look for. Although I'd like to find that brace to see if Chase stabbed him with it."

"Sure," Ben said.

"Maybe I'll go check his bedroom to see if there's any interesting stuff in there," Charlie said.

"All right." Dan handed her some markers. "If you find anything that you think needs to be collected, just mark it."

"Sure thing," she said. She made her way through the dining room, careful not to step on any of the blood on the hardwood floor. The bungalow had two bedrooms, but one had been outfitted with a large old desk and several floor-to-ceiling bookshelves. The wall across from the desk sent a shudder through her. A small table had been set up next to the wall that had been painted black with what appeared to be magnetic chalkboard paint. It had handwritten lists in chalk that Charlie couldn't decipher yet. Newspaper articles tacked to the wall with colorful plastic magnets showed pictures of an older man, probably in his mid-to-late fifties with a handlebar mustache, gray hair in the front, and long scraggly hair in the back.

"What have we got here?" Dan asked. Charlie startled. His booties had muffled his footsteps when he entered the room, and his deep voice brought her out of her deep concentration.

"Business in the front and a party in the back," Charlie said, pointing to the picture of the older man. A tattoo of a spider web stretched from the side of his neck into the tank top he wore. The photos showed several different angles of the man, including one of him shirtless, working on a car.

"What the hell?" Charlie said. She drew closer to a zoomed picture of the man's shoulder blade. A tattoo emblazoned the space. *Thou shalt not suffer a which to live ~ Exodus 22:18*

"Sweet goddess, give me strength," Charlie muttered.

"What?"

"He spelled witch wrong," Charlie pointed to the word *which* in the photo.

"Huh, imagine that. This guy really is some sort of genius, isn't he?" Dan teased.

"Oh, he's a genius all right," Charlie quipped.

"You know, from the tats in these pictures, this guy has spent time in prison."

"You can tell that just from his tattoos?" Charlie asked.

"Oh, yeah. See the teardrop tattoo on the face. That means he killed somebody in prison. Also, most reputable tattoo artists don't tattoo the face."

"Wow. Hopefully, then, he'll be easy to find," Charlie said.

"Yeah, unless he really is some sort of genius."

"He's not," Ben said, entering the office. "Hey, Athena, can you repeat that for me, please?" Ben held out his phone and tapped the speaker icon.

"Hi, Athena," Charlie said. "We're here with Dan Blankenship. He works with the Sheriff's department in this county."

"Hi, Charlie, hi, Dan," Athena chirped. "So, I ran a quick search on Matthew Goodman and came up with an interesting possibility. Matthew Ray Goodman, fifty-seven years old. He's lived all over the south from Virginia to Florida, where he spent the last nine years in prison for manslaughter. He was released about three months ago."

"Do you have any pictures of him?" Dan asked.

"I sure do," Athena said. "I'm sending his mugshots to Charlie's phone now."

A moment later, Charlie's phone vibrated. She opened the email and downloaded the pictures.

"Thanks, Athena, I've got them," Charlie said into Ben's phone.

A younger, less tattooed, less leathery-looking Matthew Goodman appeared. Charlie held up the photos on her phone and compared them to the photos on Chase's walls.

"So, interestingly," Athena said, "I ran a cross-check of unsolved witch deaths in the South that look suspicious. I overlaid it with a timeline of where Matthew Ray Goodman has lived or been in prison. There are several witch deaths that appear to be mysterious and unsolved on both the front and back of his prison sentences."

"Athena, is it?" Dan asked.

"Yes, it is," she said in her usual cheerful manner.

"That's a pretty name, by the way."

"Why, thank you. Brownie points for Dan."

Charlie chuckled. Dan's face reddened.

"I was just wondering what sort of prison sentences are we looking at? Did he commit murder or rape or assault?"

"He has been imprisoned three times. Two for aggravated assaults and once for manslaughter. He got out on good behavior for all three. Also, it looks like he was a person of interest in a murder in Tampa, Florida, in 1998."

"How on earth did you get that information," he asked.

"It looks like their files have been digitized, which

makes them searchable. I have access to pretty much all of the databases across the country for law enforcement."

"Wow. I'd ask you to marry me if I weren't already married."

Athena giggled. "I appreciate the sentiment. But I think my girlfriend might not be really happy about that."

Dan laughed awkwardly and his cheeks went from red to deep plum. "Tell your girlfriend she's a lucky lady."

"Thank you. I will let her know that," Athena said. "Is there anything else I can do for you?"

"Do you have a last known address for him?"

"I sure do. According to parole records, he's supposed to be living with his brother. I'm sending that information to both Charlie and Ben right now."

"Great job, Athena," Ben said.

"Yes, thank you, Athena," Charlie said.

"Thanks, Athena," Dan said.

Ben ended the call and opened his messaging app. "What's your number, Dan, I'm gonna forward this address to you."

Dan rattled off his phone number, and within a moment, he had the address stored safely on his phone. "That Athena is a gem."

"Yes, she is," Charlie agreed.

The sound of car doors slamming caught their attention. "Looks like your forensic team is here."

"Yep, I'm gonna go outside and get them started."

"Do you need us to stay?" Charlie asked.

"Nope. I got it from here. I can have a deputy here in a few minutes to take you back to the hotel if you want," Dan offered.

"All right, if you're sure," Charlie said.

"Yep, this is just the tedious stuff, gathering all the evidence up and cataloging it. We still have a ways to go before I can think about arresting the dude."

"Yeah," Charlie said.

Ben shook Dan's hand and then said, "Come on, Charlie, I think I have something else we can do today. At least till Dan needs us again. Thanks again, Dan."

"No problem. Thank y'all. This is gonna go a long way to building a case."

"Anytime," Charlie said.

CHAPTER 26

"In three hundred feet, turn left onto Heron Circle." The pleasant semi-robotic voice filled Evangeline's car. She squinted at the small screen of her phone trying to make sense of the colorful GPS map. Personally, she preferred paper maps. They were concrete, something she could touch. She even liked the crinkly noise they made when she tried to fold them back into their original neat, crisp shape. She sighed. Paper maps weren't practical when driving, especially not in the traffic from Palmetto Point to Daniel Island, where Scott Carver lived.

"In three hundred feet, your destination will be on the right."

"That's good," she said to her phone, then felt silly for speaking to it.

"You have arrived at your destination," the voice said, completing the instructions. Evangeline pulled her little truck into the driveway of Scott Carver's large luxurious home.

Evangeline leaned forward to examine the three-story, Victorian-style house. It was easily close to four thousand square feet. She clucked her tongue, glad she didn't have to clean it.

The empty porch caught her attention, disapproval darkening her eyes. She should've known Scott might pull something at the change of plans; she just wasn't sure what he had up his sleeve. They had agreed, when she'd called him to arrange to pick up Evan, that the boy would wait on the porch with his backpack and things at 3:00 p.m. sharp. Evangeline checked the time on her old Timex watch. Yes, right on time.

"Damn it, Scott," she muttered. For one second, she thought of just beeping the horn. That would yank his chain. She chuckled, and then thought better of it.

Her niece's ex-husband could be aggressively controlling, especially when it came to his ex-wife. Charlie Payne tended to throw curveballs at Scott. Evangeline understood that probably more than even Scott understood it himself.

The last thing she wanted was for Scott to give Charlie a hard time. Evangeline suspected Charlie was having a hard enough time as it was. She didn't need to add to her niece's burden. She plucked the keys from the ignition and tucked them into the pocket of her jeans once she stepped out of her little truck. When she reached the large oak double doors with the stained-glass windows, she peered through one of the clear panes. Why wasn't Evan waiting inside? Once she rang the bell, it took a couple of minutes for Scott to open the door.

"Evangeline." He gave her a curt nod. In his khaki pants and blue Oxford open-necked shirt, his regal good-looks reminded Evangeline why Charlie had been so smitten with him all those years ago. His hazel eyes looked her up and down. "It's been a long time."

"Yes, it has," Evangeline said. "Is Evan ready?"

"He'll be along in a moment. Won't you come in?"

Evangeline smiled but gave him a sharp look. "No, thank you. I'll wait on the porch. Like we agreed."

"Suit yourself. I was just offering you a chance to get out of the weather."

Evangeline glanced around at the sun-drenched yard and street. According to the Channel 5 news, the temperature was supposed to get up to seventy-two degrees. The first warm day all month. She hadn't even bothered to wear a jacket. Just a long-sleeved, pink flannel blouse tucked into her jeans.

"That's very thoughtful. I mean look at that sun. It's so..." She didn't hold back. "Sunny."

Scott scowled and rolled his eyes before he called up the staircase. "Evan! Your great aunt is here."

"Thank you." Evangeline folded her arms across her chest and walked to the porch railing with the long line of azaleas at the front of the house. She could see tight little buds, the beginning of the new foliage. In a few weeks' time, azaleas all over the low country would explode with her favorite bright colors of magenta, pink, red, and white, and she couldn't wait.

Scott stepped out onto the porch and closed the door behind him before he sidled up next to her.

"Just so you know his routine," Scott began. "Evan gets out of school at 2:45. He takes the bus home, does his homework with my housekeeper Cora in the afternoons, and she feeds him around 5:00 p.m. Usually, on Charlie's weeks, she picks him up around six. Although, lately it's been closer to seven," he grumbled.

"Evan's not a little child anymore," Evangeline said. "Does he really need such a strict routine?"

"Routines are good. If I left it to Charlie, he might not eat dinner till seven or eight."

"True, but I'm not Charlie. I'll just pick him up from school myself, instead of him taking the bus. I'll bring him to my house with me. I'll make sure he gets his homework done in the afternoons, and we'll eat by six," Evangeline said.

"Yes, but—"

"But what?" Evangeline met Scott's gaze. "He'll still get his homework done and be fed at a reasonable time."

Scott opened his mouth and closed it a few times. It reminded Evangeline of a fish stranded on the beach. She almost enjoyed the emotions that played out across his face. He seemed to argue with himself silently.

He wouldn't dare argue with her. Evangeline had met his mother and she knew he'd been raised not to be rude or disrespectful. He could give Charlie a hard time all he wanted. They'd been married. But giving Evangeline a hard time wouldn't go well.

"Fine. If he gets his homework done. That's all I care about."

"He will."

"So... have you heard from Charlie?" Scott asked.

"I have. She texted me yesterday and asked me to pick up Evan."

"How much do you know about her job?"

"Enough. She enjoys what she's doing, and from what Ben says, she's good at it."

"Who's Ben?"

"Her boss," Evangeline said. "She's happy, Scott. And that's all I care about."

"Yes. But it's dangerous, right? And all this travel..." Scott muttered.

"Whenever you deal with other people, there's danger involved. I don't care who you are." She shook her head.

"Anything can happen at any time to anyone, Scott. You'll drive yourself crazy if you think about it too much. It'll keep you from living your life."

"Yes, but I'm not just living for me. And some jobs are much safer than others. She was never in such danger when she worked at the call center."

Evangeline opened her mouth to argue. Had he forgotten Charlie had been attacked in the parking lot of her call center? Or, had she just not told him? She closed her mouth.

"Well, take heart. Charlie is a very good witch and has more resources at her disposal than most because of her employer. I'm not gonna say don't worry. But I am going to say that you should trust her. She knows what she's doing," Evangeline said.

"Sure," Scott said.

"So, Charlie says you have a new girlfriend," Evangeline said.

Scott scowled. "Did she?"

Evangeline raised one eyebrow. "She did. I think it's good. I'm glad that you have somebody in your life."

"Thank you," Scott said. His cheeks flushed with pink.

A moment later, the door opened, and Evan came out carrying a duffel bag in one hand, and his backpack slung over one shoulder.

"Evangeline," he said with a big smile plastered across his face. "It's good to see you." He dropped the duffel bag and wrapped his arm around his great aunt's waist.

"I swear you grow an inch every time I turn around." Evangeline hugged him close. "It won't be long before you're as tall as your mama."

From the corner of her eye, she saw Scott's nose wrinkle and suppressed a chuckle. He'd always been a little sensitive about his height, especially when it came to Charlie. His ex-wife stood a good half-inch above him when she slouched, and more than an inch when she stood up straight.

"Yeah," Evan agreed. "You ready to go?"

"Do you have everything?"

"Yes, ma'am, I do," he said.

"Then we better be on our way. Jen is expecting us for dinner tonight."

"Great," he said. "I love Jen's cooking." Evan started for the steps.

"Evan?" Scott called.

Evan stopped in his tracks.

"You're not gonna say goodbye to me?"

"Oh, right. Bye, Dad. See you next week." Evan waved and then rushed down the steps and loaded his things into the back of Evangeline's truck.

Evangeline patted Scott on the shoulder. "Don't worry. It's just part of being a teenager. It'll get better."

"When?" Scott said.

"In about ten years," Evangeline said.

"Evan will be out of college by then," Scott said.

"Yes, I know." Evangeline grinned and gave him a wink. "You have a great week, and don't worry so much. I'll have him text you every day."

"Thanks." Scott didn't leave the front porch until the two of them got into her truck and pulled out of the driveway, heading home to Palmetto Point.

CHAPTER 27

"So, what's our plan, Ben?" Charlie said as the deputy dropped the trio in front of the hotel.

"Let's get up to our rooms first. I need to check in with Jen and pay a visit to a man."

Charlie smiled and said, "Gotcha," as she and Tom exited the vehicle.

"There she is," Charlie said, nudging Ben. She waved to Jen and Lisa standing near the potted palm at the reception desk in the cozy hotel lobby. "Our welcoming committee."

"Why are they decked out in shorts and flip-flops and carrying beach towels?" Ben asked sounding a little wooden. The sisters crossed the lobby and met them half-way.

"Where are y'all going?" Charlie asked.

Jen held up her towel and beach bag. "What does it look like? We're going to the beach. We want you to come with us," she said. Her gaze went around the circle of faces. "All of y'all."

"I don't know." Charlie fidgeted with her cast. "Dan is supposed to call and let me know if they're going to arrest Matthew Goodman or not today."

"Come on, Charlie, you heard him," Ben said. "They'll probably be at Chase's most of the day gathering and documenting the evidence. And it sounded like it's gonna take a while. I doubt he's gonna call you today. Doubt he's gonna call this week, honestly," Ben said.

Charlie gave him a side-eyed glance. "Are you in on this?"

Ben held his hands up in surrender. "I may have been in on the brainstorming."

"What does that mean?" Charlie asked.

"It means we're going to see an energy healer about a former psychic we know and love," Lisa said. "Now go upstairs, put on some shorts and flip-flops, and let's all go to the beach."

"It's kind of cold to go to the beach, isn't it?" Charlie asked.

"It's supposed to be seventy-five today," Lisa countered. "And nobody said anything about getting in the water."

"You don't have to put on shorts if you'd rather stay in

your jeans and hoodie. But regardless, you're going to the beach with us." Jen glanced at the stainless steel watch on her wrist. "We're supposed to meet an energy healer there in about thirty minutes."

"Fine." Charlie didn't hide her irritation. "But I want it noted for the record that I feel a little ambushed here."

"So, noted." Jen gave her a brief nod. "Now, let's go."

Charlie's cousins marched her out of the hotel, and the five of them piled into Ben's Toyota FJ50 and headed toward the beach.

It took them over half an hour to drive through a string of beach towns with houses on stilts, surf shops, and boat storage marinas before they reached their desti-nation. Ben pulled into a sandy gravel parking lot with a bank of dunes on either side of a boardwalk entrance to the beach. Only a few other cars were parked in the small lot, and Ben had his choice of spots close to the boardwalk.

A tall, dark-haired woman in a patterned multi-colored maxi dress stood tall at the entrance to the one-story address Ben had plugged into his GPS. From her long curly hair tied back in a scarf to her incandescent tawny skin that glowed in the early afternoon sun, every-thing about the woman emanated strength, calm, and wisdom. Her chiseled features made Charlie think of stone carvings of goddesses. Her stomach flip-flopped, and her breath caught in her throat. What was she getting herself into?

She slipped out of the truck, feeling wary but curious. After all, she trusted her cousins, didn't she? Ben waved as they approached the woman, looking regal as her terra cotta-colored lips stretched into a wide smile.

"Esperanza?" Jen called.

"Yes." Esperanza nodded. The tail of her headscarf whipped in the wind.

"Hi, I'm Jen Holloway. We spoke on the phone." Jen extended her hand, and Esperanza took it, wrapping both of her hands around Jen's.

"So nice to meet you," she said. Her dark eyes focused on Jen's face.

Jen motioned for Charlie to come forward. "This is my cousin, Charlie Payne. The one I told you about."

"Oh, yes," she said. Esperanza's intense gaze shifted to Charlie's face. "You're the one investigating Ariel Martin's death."

"That's right." Charlie stepped up next to Jen, rocked on her heels and fought the urge to just run away.

"I'm Esperanza Guzman. I'm the High Priestess for the covens in this area."

Charlie narrowed her eyes. "You were on my list to question."

"Yes. It's such a tragic loss for our coven. She was so young and had so many dreams. Such beautiful energy."

"Yes, it is," Charlie said. She didn't mention Chase. His family hadn't been notified yet, and Charlie thought since it was Dan's case, he should be the one to regulate the ebb and flow of information to the public. "I can't say much, but we do have a strong suspect in the case."

Esperanza reached for Charlie's good hand and took it into both of hers. "That is wonderful news. Her family will be so relieved." Esperanza did not take her eyes off her. Charlie wanted to burrow into her hoodie to hide from such scrutiny. "Come with me. Let's take a walk on the beach."

Charlie glanced over her shoulder toward her cousins. "Should they come too? Or—"

"No. This work is for you and me to do." She wrapped her arm around Charlie's shoulders and guided her toward the beach. They walked to the end of the board-walk, and at the end of the ramp, Charlie slipped her tennis shoes off and let her feet sink into the soft, white sand. The beach stretched for miles in both directions, and only a few joggers dotted the shoreline.

She wiggled her toes, relishing the coolness of the sand. The wind whipped around them, and even though the sun warmed her face, Charlie shivered, glad she'd worn her hoodie. It had been a while since she'd been on a beach. If she had to be honest with herself, she'd been avoiding it. She breathed in, and the salt air coated her tongue. She closed her eyes, and for the first time since she'd lost her abilities, her whole body relaxed.

"That's good." Esperanza patted Charlie's arm. "Drink it in. I've always found this place very healing."

Charlie agreed and took a few more deep breaths. "Do you think the water's cold?"

"Probably a little cold, but if you want to dip your toes in, we can walk down to the edge of the water."

Charlie wrinkled her nose and shook her head. A flash of the day she almost died slipped into her mind. They'd packed her in ice to chill her body to hypothermic temperatures. "We can just walk. I don't like cold water."

"Fair enough. Let's walk." Esperanza hooked her arm in Charlie's and guided her down to the harder sand, which made walking easier. After a few moments, Esperanza broke the silence between them. "You've been carrying a very heavy burden, and you've pushed everyone away because of it."

"Did Jen tell you that?"

"Your cousin mentioned that you had a near-death experience."

"I did."

"And it was life-altering." Esperanza stopped and gently turned Charlie to face her. "Which is what's caused your block."

"My block?" Charlie asked.

"Yes, Charlie. You have not lost your abilities. They're still with you. Still part of you."

Charlie shook her head and grabbed her arm above her cast with her good hand. "It certainly feels like they're gone."

"Trust me. I've been evaluating and healing other people's energy for many, many years. Most of the time, when some trusted part of us stops working, it's because something is blocking the flow of energy within."

"And you think I'm blocked?" Charlie said.

"Oh, I know you are." Esperanza chuckled. "I can see it. That is *my* sight."

"Of course." Charlie slapped her forehead. "I should've realized it. My cousins Lisa and Daphne can read people's energies."

"Healing your energy will not be a fast process. It will take work on your part, but it can be done." Esperanza reached into the pocket of her dress and withdrew two crystals. She held them out to Charlie—a striated, pale blue crystal of a type she'd never seen before, and a darker one, marbled blue with flecks of brown, gold, and white—both tumbled to a smooth, highly polished sheen that glinted in the sunlight. Esperanza pointed to the striated stone.

"This is Blue Kyanite. Lie on the floor when you meditate and place it here." She pointed to her forehead, centered a little above her brows. "The other is Sodalite. Place both under your pillow at night. Do this every day."

"Until my abilities return?"

"No." Esperanza smiled wide and placed her hand on Charlie's upper arm. "This will be an ongoing process for the rest of your life."

"Okay. Forever's a really long time." Charlie took the crystals in her hand and stared at them, letting their energy flow into her for a few seconds before she dropped them into the front pocket of her jeans.

"Healing our energy is continuous," Esperanza said.

Charlie blew out a breath and nodded. "Is that all I have to do?"

"No. You must talk."

"Talk about—"

"Talk about your anger. Your resentment."

Charlie shook her head in disagreement. "I'm not angry."

"Charlie, you are angry. And resentful and..." Esperanza's eyes narrowed. Charlie hated feeling like a bug being studied in a jar. She kept waiting for a pin to poke her as if someone intended to mount her on a piece of foam core for a science project. "And very sad about what you think you lost."

"What I did lose," Charlie snapped. "I lost an eternity of this." She gestured to the beach around them. "And...I lost...there aren't words enough to explain the sheer love that flowed through me. Enveloped me really. It was like music."

"A higher vibration." Esperanza tipped her head, understanding as no one else ever had. "Yes. I can see that too. You were touched by the divine, and strangely, that is a hard thing to recover from."

Tears stung Charlie's eyes. "Is it terrible that I want to go back?"

"No, child. It is not terrible." Esperanza wrapped her arms around Charlie and drew her into a hug. Charlie folded herself into the woman's embrace. The tears ripped through her like a storm, and she was powerless to stop them.

"Grief is normal," Esperanza whispered against her ear. "This higher divinity is now part of you, Charlie. Something you will always carry with you. And here is something else I want you to think about." Esperanza hugged her with a force that seemed to expunge some of her grief. "You came back because you still have things to do in this realm. Your purpose is here for now."

"But I don't want it to be." Charlie choked out the words. It was the first time she'd admitted this to herself, and guilt flooded through her, bringing with it another wave of tears.

"I know. But until you accept it, you will remain blocked from your true purpose." Esperanza pulled away from Charlie enough to cup her face. "Do you understand?"

"How do I do that?"

"The first thing you should do is going to sound painful. But it must be done."

"What is it?" Charlie asked.

"I want you to write out a list of five reasons you're grateful for still being in this plane of existence."

Charlie sniffled and straightened. The wetness on her skin chilled her cheeks, and she wiped it away with the cuff of her sweatshirt. "All right. I can try."

Esperanza gently scolded her. "No. As Yoda said, there is no try."

Charlie laughed, and the vibration it made in her chest chased away the lingering sadness for now. "Great. I'm being advised by the teachings of Yoda."

"There is wisdom everywhere, Charlie. Even in a Star Wars movie," Esperanza teased.

"Okay. I'll write my list."

"Good. And don't be surprised if you are suddenly flooded by your abilities one day, and they slow to a trickle the next. It's all part of restoring the flow of energy."

Charlie nodded. "Can I call you for advice if I need to?"

"Yes, of course. I was actually going to suggest we meet weekly until your block has resolved itself."

"How are we gonna do that? I'll probably go home this week," Charlie said.

Esperanza patted her arm. "We'll video chat."

Charlie threw her head back and let out an embarrassed laugh. "Of course! I should've thought of that."

CHAPTER 28

"So, Evangeline." Evan sat back in his chair. They were having dinner at the small dining table next to the kitchen in Evangeline's condo. "What kind of magic are we gonna focus on this week? I was really thinking about trying to find a money spell. Do you think you could help me with it?"

Evangeline was loading her fork with roasted chicken and au gratin potatoes. "What do you need money for, Evan?"

Evan leaned forward and put his elbows on the table. "There's this necklace that I want for my girlfriend, Rachel. At the crystal shop you took me to that time. Our three-month anniversary is coming up, so I wanted to get her something special."

"I thought you got an allowance, sweetie?" Evangeline gave him a puzzled look.

Evan shifted in his chair and pushed the potatoes on his plate around with his fork. "I usually do, but I've asked for a few advances since I met Rachel, and my dad says I'm not gonna get my allowance again until June."

"I see," Evangeline put her fork down on her plate. "Do you remember how we talked about respecting magic and not trying to game it for our own gain?"

"Yes, ma'am," Evan said. He took a long drink of milk, avoiding Evangeline's stare.

"And do you remember how we talked about how magic is really about your energy. Your thoughts and your intentions."

"Yes ma'am." He put his glass down and picked up his fork, squirming a bit in his chair, his T-shirt feeling a bit tight around his neck.

"Money magic is really rooted in gratitude. Do you know what that means?"

"That I have to be grateful for the magic?" Evan asked.

"No, honey, you have to be grateful for what you already have. That's what it means. And intentions about money require extreme specificity."

Now Evan focused his full gaze on his aunt. "What does that mean, specificity?"

Evangeline's hair had slipped out of her clip, and she tucked it behind her ear. "It means, let's say that you want to earn enough money to buy your mother a birthday present."

"Or my girlfriend a necklace."

"All right, or your girlfriend a necklace. It means that you need to think about the exact amount of money that you need to earn. Focus on that intention. See that money already in your hand."

"Yeah?" Evan shifted in his seat with excitement at the thought of just imagining money appearing in his hand.

"Then you know what you have to do?"

"No, what?"

"You have to make a sacrifice."

"What do you mean?" His eagerness turned to fear, curdling his enthusiasm. "Sacrifice what?" he asked warily.

Evangeline smoothed her napkin in her lap after dabbing at a ring of condensation Evan's glass had left on the table. "Your time. Your energy. You must work for it, Evan. There's no magic shortcut to bringing lots of money into your life. Oh, there are spells. But they can sometimes take a long time, and it sounds like you have an immediate need."

"Yeah I do. I was hoping it would be faster."

"I see," Evangeline said. "Well, if you want to earn some money, I can definitely use you in the café after school. I'm a little shorthanded right now since Jen is out of town."

"Like what kind of work?" Evan said. "And don't forget that I have basketball on Wednesdays after school."

"Yes, I remember. I think you told me like five times. You can certainly bus tables and help refill things like the napkin dispensers, ketchups, and salt and pepper shakers. There's plenty of work for you to do."

"And you would pay me?"

"Yes. I would pay you a dollar above minimum wage for every hour that you work. You would basically earn $8.25 an hour."

"$8.25?" Evan asked.

"That's correct."

"It's not a lot of money. I mean, it would take me weeks to earn what that necklace costs. It's almost $200."

"Yes, my dear it will. That's exactly how the real world works."

"Fine. I'll think about it." He sighed. "So, what kind of magic are we going to work on this week?"

"I'm afraid we're not. Since Jen is out of town, I've got to run the restaurant, and I'll be very busy. I promise, once Jen gets home, we can work on some spells, all right? Some age-appropriate spells."

Evan stabbed his potatoes with his fork, and the tines clinked against the porcelain. "Fine." He took a bite. Why did Jen have to go to Florida to see his mother? A frightening thought filled his head, and he couldn't shake it.

"Evangeline, who's taking care of Poe while my mom and Jen are out of town?"

"Your Uncle Jack is."

The way she said it made him think she believed it would comfort him, but it didn't. "I didn't think he liked animals. Especially not cats."

"That's not true. He used to have this old chocolate lab that he loved. This is before you were born, though. He took that dog everywhere. He was never the same after that dog died. He swore he'd never have another one. Claimed it was too much work, but I think it broke his heart. Don't let him fool you. He loves animals."

"Okay, as long as she's okay."

"She'll be fine. If you want, we can drop by this week, and you can play with her."

"That'd be great. Thank you."

"Good, now finish your dinner. We have an early day tomorrow, and I'd like to get to bed by nine."

Evan raised his eyebrows and took the last two bites of his potatoes. Rachel had warned him that old people like to go to bed early. Even his mom didn't go to bed till 10:30 most nights. "Is it okay if I stay up? I usually don't go to bed that early."

"Really? Maybe I should text your father and ask him what your bedtime is. Could you get me my purse? It's over on the chair near the door."

"No, that's okay," Evan said. "I can go to bed early. I'm

just not used to going to bed so early, that's all. It will be nice to get some extra z's."

"Yes, I'm sure it will, especially since you're a growing boy. Your body needs lots of sleep."

"Yeah. Of course." Evan frowned at his plate.

"You finished with your dinner?" Evangeline asked.

"Yes, ma'am."

"Wonderful. Then you can help me with the dishes. I'll wash, and you can dry."

"Great." Evan rolled his eyes at her back and got up from his seat, trying to remember why he'd thought staying with his great aunt would be so much fun.

CHAPTER 29

Bright and early Wednesday morning, Charlie sat at the small table in her hotel room and took another stab at her gratitude list. So far, she had the following:

1. Evan

2. Tom

3. Job at the DOL

She wanted to be grateful for her cousins and the rest of her family. She loved them, and they loved her. She'd had their support through everything, but some part of her blamed them for... for? She couldn't put her finger on it, but shouldn't they have stepped in sooner or used their powers to stop what had happened to her? She didn't know. Which she knew was totally unfair. But still. If honesty was the word of the day, yeah, she was pissed at them, in addition to loving them to death.

She still couldn't add their names to her gratitude list, so she closed her notebook and shoved it back into her purse. She glanced around the empty hotel room. Tom was out patrolling the grounds, and Ben was in his room. She relished the rare quiet.

Lisa and Jason had rented a car Monday, and along with Jen, returned home. But Charlie and Ben had stayed, hoping that Dan would gather enough evidence to arrest Matthew Goodman. Jason had spotted him on security footage going into the lobby of Charlie's hotel, but the video of the restaurant parking lot had only revealed someone parking Chase's car and a man in a hooded sweatshirt getting out and walking away. He never looked up, and although his body type could have passed for Matthew Goodman, Dan couldn't say for sure.

She pulled out her phone and jotted off a quick text to Ben. Maybe they could head over to the Sheriff's station to see if they could be of any use. All this waiting around made her antsy. She stared at the screen for a moment waiting for a response, but none came.

Charlie picked up the blue Kyanite crystal sitting on the table next to her purse. She traced the slight striations with her thumb and found the motion soothing. A moment later, she hopped up from her seat and eased down on the bed, still moving gingerly because of her cast. She placed the stone on her forehead just as Esperanza had shown her. So far, her meditations had not yielded much. A flash of light here. Familiar sounds and smells there. But nothing cohesive. Nothing like before.

Charlie closed her eyes, relaxed her body, and let her good arm fall next to her side. She had a habit of clutching the cast, so she let it go and concentrated on the rising and falling of her chest, the feeling of air entering and exiting her nostrils. Every muscle relaxed, and she drifted into a place she liked to call her gray space. Her thoughts drifted in, and she batted them away. This was the place where visions and dreams were born.

"Charlie, girl?" A familiar voice echoed through her mind.

"Bunny?" Charlie called.

"Who else would it be?" Her grandmother's face appeared in her head, full of light and good humor. Her blue eyes twinkled, and she smiled, looking younger than Charlie ever remembered her in life.

"I have missed you so much, Bunny," Charlie said.

"I've been trying to get through to you and to visit you in your dreams, but you've been locked up tight, young lady."

"I know. I'm sorry. I'm working on it."

"That's all that matters. I noticed a shift this morning and wanted to pop in and tell you I love you," she said.

"I love you, too, Bunny." A pang of sorrow filled her

chest. "I just feel like I've been flying blind for the last couple of months."

"You're only blind because you've closed your eyes, my darling girl. You have to open your eyes."

"I know," Charlie whispered. "But I'm scared."

"There's nothing to fear. Not there and not here. We are always waiting for you, my darling girl."

"Bunny, can you tell me the truth about something?"

"Yes, if you ask me directly, I will answer you truthfully," Bunny said.

"Did a witchfinder kill my parents and Aunt Ellen?"

Bunny laughed. "Whoohoo, someone's been telling tall tales. Or, maybe it's just been wishful thinking on their part. Something to get under your skin, and make you focus on the wrong thing."

"The wrong thing?" Charlie repeated.

"Yes, my darling."

"And what is the right thing?" Charlie asked.

"The right thing would be the root of the manipulation. How the information was used at all."

"I don't understand," Charlie said.

"Open your eyes, Charlie. Open your eyes, and your heart, and your mind, and all the answers will be yours." Bunny grinned. "Almost time to start planting my garden, so I need to head back. Just remember who you are."

"Who am I?" Charlie asked.

"You, my darling, are a powerful witch from a long

line of powerful witches. We are all standing behind you."

"Thank you, Bunny," Charlie whispered.

"Please give Evangeline, Jen, Lisa, and Daphne my love."

"I will," Charlie said. Her grandmother's face gently floated into the gray space and faded. Charlie opened her eyes.

How had Matthew Goodman known anything about her parents' death? He'd even misspelled her name in the note. The only mention of her in her parents' obituaries that she could remember had referred to her as Charlotte —not Charlie. Then she remembered Athena saying something about information being deleted from Ariel Martin's file.

Charlie opened her eyes.

"He's working with somebody at the DOL."

The sound of her voice startled her, and she sat up. The crystal fell from the center of her forehead, and she caught it with her good hand. She couldn't wait for Ben anymore. She quickly texted Athena.

Please call me.

Less than a minute later, her phone vibrated on the table.

"Hey, Charlie," Athena said. "How's it going?"

"It's just a waiting game at this point."

"Sure. Worst part."

"I have a question for you, Athena."

"Shoot."

"Who else can access the databases like you do?"

"Let's see, Charlie. Whole departments have access. Security can do it. Information Technology can do it. And, of course, anybody in the Investigations Unit. Why?"

"Because I think we have a mole."

"What do you mean?" Athena asked. Charlie pictured her when she got riled up, leaning across her desk as if climbing into her phone.

Charlie laid out her theory that Matthew Goodman had access to someone at the DOL. Someone with the ability to search the databases for background and the whereabouts of witches.

"Holy mother goddess," Athena said in a breathy voice. "If that's true, we're all exposed."

"Yeah, we are. And I don't think it's gonna stop with Matthew Goodman. What if there are more like him? More witchfinders?"

Athena clucked her tongue. "Holy...That's gonna take some work to figure out. I mean, we'll have to come up with... I don't know how many variables."

"Take a breath. We don't have to do it today, Athena. But I want you to be thinking about it because I trust you. And I know how smart you are."

"Aww. Thank you. I appreciate that. You're smart too."

Charlie chuckled. "Let's just hope I'm getting smarter. You start working on a way for us to set a trap."

"This could take a while," Athena said. Charlie imagined her scratching her head and red curls falling around her ears. "We should probably let Ben in on it. And when you guys get back, we can sit down and have a meeting, just the three of us."

"Sounds like a plan."

"Great. I'll start making some lists," Athena said with her usual enthusiasm.

"Great. Just make sure you keep all of it to yourself."

"Absolutely. My lips are sealed. And I will cast a glamour over any of my notes."

"Great idea. Talk to you later."

"You bet, Charlie," Athena said and ended the call.

Charlie stared down at her phone, wondering who to call next and jumped a little when it vibrated in her hand. The sight of Dan's name sent a fresh wave of flutters through her stomach.

"Dan!" Charlie said. "I was going to call you."

"I guess we're on the same wavelength. That's a thing right, wavelength?"

Charlie laughed. "It is, actually. But it's more of a scientific principle than a witch thing. But in either case, it works. "

He laughed, and the warm sound made Charlie laugh, too.

"So, we're on our way to arrest Matthew Goodman."

"Are you serious?" Charlie asked.

"Yes, I am. How would you like to sit in on an interview?"

"Nothing on this earth could make me happier," Charlie said. "Except maybe a dead vampire."

"We'll work on that one next," Dan chuckled. "Can you meet me at the Sheriff's station in about an hour?"

"Hell, yeah. I will be there with bells on." Charlie hung up and laughed like a giddy schoolgirl. Then she slipped on her tennis shoes and went down the hall to find Ben and Tom.

CHAPTER 30

Charlie and Ben crammed into the small A/V room with the technician and Dan. Tom said he'd rather guard the perimeter of the building than watch the interview, which Charlie secretly preferred.

The three of them stared at the monitor. The camera in the interview room was centered on Matthew Goodman. Dan had cuffed him during the arrest, and after getting the resistant suspect into one of the metal chairs, Dan had secured the cuffs to the metal table. Every few minutes, Goodman looked at the camera and made a devilish face, sticking out his long, pointed tongue and growling.

"We have ways to compel him to talk," Ben said softly.

Charlie gave the technician a side-eyed glance to see if he had noticed.

"Yeah," Dan said, "so do we, but that's not the problem. The problem is he already said, 'I want a lawyer'. Now, if you can get him to take that back," Dan added, raising his brows in a suggestive grimace, "I'm all for it."

"I bet I could do it," Charlie said. "Without having to resort to..." She gave Ben a pointed look. "You know."

"What are you thinking?" Dan asked.

"Why don't you and I go sit in there and chat," she said. "He doesn't have to talk to us. But that doesn't mean he can't listen to us talk to each other."

"All right, I see where you're going with this."

"I don't know," Ben said. "I don't think I like this. It's not safe for you to go in there, Charlie. At least not here. I mean, if we were at our offices that would be different. We would have ways to secure him where he could not physically come at you. I mean, that table's not even bolted to the floor."

Charlie gave Ben her stubborn face. "Dan will be with me," she insisted, keeping her gaze level, like a steel poker. "You've seen Dan, right? He's like a brick wall." She gestured to Dan. "And I'll take my..." Her eyes darted to the technician whose head was cocked toward them, trying to listen in, of that she was certain. "You know I'll be fine," she said, forcing a pleasant tone for the benefit of the eavesdropper.

"At least let me..." Ben frowned when Charlie flicked her eyes to the technician. "Is there someplace we can go and talk freely?" he said under his breath.

"Sure, come on. The other interview room is empty." Dan led them out of the A/V room and down the hall to the room where Charlie had questioned Chase Andrews.

"Is that on?" Ben pointed to the camera.

"No. There's no light on," Dan said.

"Great. Charlie, I know you want to go in there and just shred this guy. But I really am worried about your safety. You have a broken hand. If anything ever happened to you, let's just say your whole family would never forgive me. And I'm not even gonna mention Tom."

"You just did." Charlie smirked. "I appreciate your concern. And I understand that dealing with my family is a formidable thing, but we can't let it get in the way of making sure this guy goes to jail."

"Fine. But would you at least let me cast a repelling spell?"

"What is that?" Dan asked.

"It's basically so he can't touch me. But don't forget," she said, slanting a look at Ben, "it makes it hard for me to touch him, too."

"Why would you want to touch him?" Dan and Ben said at the same time.

"I'm getting little flashes of things since my meeting

with Esperanza. Maybe I'll see something that will provoke him into confessing."

"I don't want you touching him." Ben shook his head. "No way."

"Yeah, I'm gonna have to go with Ben on this. I don't think that's a good idea," Dan said. "Because when he finally does talk to a lawyer, they could use it against us."

"I don't want to do anything to ruin the case." Charlie scowled, filled with profound disappointment, "Okay, Ben, cast the spell."

"Great." Ben reached into the messenger bag he always wore across his body and pulled out a black velvet pouch. He opened it and plucked out an obsidian crystal. "Put this in your pocket."

Charlie did as he asked. He moved close, put one hand on her shoulder and held the other in front of her heart.

"You don't have a wand?" Dan asked.

"No. I don't use one. My hands are just as good as a wand. Maybe better," Ben said.

"That is debatable," Charlie quipped. "But we don't have time for it right now."

Ben ignored the taunt and said, "Close your eyes."

Charlie did as he asked, and within seconds, felt the energy flowing from his right hand into her shoulder and the energy from his other hand pouring into her chest. The pulses of energy flowed through her, and she imagined them connecting like an electrical circuit. Her fingertips tingled, and her ears rang, drowning out Ben's whispers of the spell.

"So, mote it be," Ben said.

The ringing and tingling stopped. Charlie opened her eyes. "Is it specific to him? And how long is it going to last?"

"It's specific to evil men and evil creatures. Maybe a few days at most," Ben said. "I'm hoping that if you have to encounter the vampire again, it will work against him as well. But if you're worried about Tom or someone else you love touching you, don't. It doesn't apply to us."

"All right. Good. Let's do this."

CHARLIE AND MATTHEW GOODMAN ENGAGED IN A STARING contest across the table. His thick mustache twitched with the smirk on his lips. Tattoos crept up his neck from beneath the neckline of his shirt and the mullet he wore emphasized the squareness of his large head. For the first time in two months, beyond normal empathy, she could actually feel another human being's emotions. His hatred rolled off him in waves. She had never been so happy to sense such an undercurrent of animosity and disgust in her life.

"So, Charlie," Dan said, drawing her attention away

from the malevolent smile on Goodman's face. "What're your plans after this?"

"I plan to go home and see my son and my family. Ostara is coming up next month, so we'll be planning a big celebration."

Goodman made a disgusted noise.

"So, what is Ostara again?" Dan asked.

"It's a pagan celebration of the vernal equinox. My cousins and I decorate with all things spring. Then we boil eggs, color them, and hide them for the kids. My cousin always has a big feast to welcome spring."

"Sounds a lot like Easter," Dan said.

"Well, sure," Charlie said. "A lot of current holiday customs—"

"Sounds like the devil's work if you ask me," Goodman said.

"No one asked you," Dan said. "You invoked your right to counsel, which means you need to shut your mouth."

Charlie pressed her lips together to keep from smiling.

"Unless you *want* to talk," Charlie said. "And I distinctly get the feeling that you want to talk."

"You have nothing on me," Goodman said.

"Yeah, well, unless you want to talk about it without your lawyer present, I'm going to urge you to shut your mouth," Dan said. Charlie glanced at Dan. She liked his tough demeanor. She turned to Goodman and gave him a coy smile this time, not holding back her glee.

"You were saying, Charlie?"

"We always have a good time, like most of our holidays. You should come up for the summer solstice. We have a huge bonfire, and my cousin makes the best barbecue you have ever tasted. It's so much fun. You'd really enjoy it."

"It sounds interesting," Dan said. "You're the first pagan I've ever known."

"You mean witch. Or should I say, bitch," Goodman said.

"Watch your mouth!" Dan snapped. Charlie touched his arm.

"It's okay, Dan. I am a witch, and I come from a long line of powerful witches. What of it?" she said.

"Charlie, he can't talk to us."

"That's right. Because if he did, he wouldn't be able to control himself. He'd want to brag about what he's done. So, it's probably the smart move for him to keep his mouth shut. Assuming he can keep his mouth shut," Charlie said.

"Yeah, well, so far, that's a big assumption," Dan said.

Matthew Goodman glared at her. "I didn't do anything wrong."

"Why don't you talk to us then?" Dan asked. "Don't you know only guilty people ask for lawyers?"

"Ain't guilty of shit. I'm doing the Lord's work."

"You can't discuss what kind of work you're doing unless you waive your right to counsel. I'm not gonna tell you to shut your mouth again," Dan said.

"You would've already booked me if you had anything on me."

"Maybe so," Charlie said. "Or maybe we're just letting your partner tell us everything."

Goodman's smug expression evaporated. "What partner?"

"You know, the one from the DOL. The one who was feeding you information. Or maybe you were his puppet. We have him in a room at the DOL, right now. I'm sure he'll tell us the situation. Giving us all the information we need on you. So, you're right. It's probably better that you don't talk to us."

"I don't have a partner, bitch."

"Hey! I'm not gonna say it again," Dan warned.

"I think you do, and I think he's setting you up to take the fall for everything. Making sure we know that it was all your idea to hunt witches."

"Hell, I've been hunting witches since he was a twinkle in his daddy's eye. You tell that little shit that I will gut him if he says one word."

"I'm not sure what you don't understand about your right to silence when you invoke counsel," Dan said. "But you need to either shut up or talk to us. Because he is talking, and that means we're gonna take his word over yours."

"Screw that!" Goodman said. "I want whatever deal he's getting."

"Okay. And you'll revoke your request for counsel?" Dan asked.

"Hell, yeah."

"Done," Charlie said. She eyed the fresh bandage on Goodman's upper arm.

"The first thing I want to know is, did you kill Ariel Martin and Chase Andrews?" Dan asked.

"Yep. I killed them with their own medicine."

"Is that how you got that wound?" Charlie leaned forward.

Goodman looked down at his arm. "Yeah, that little witch boy broke a chair and jabbed me with it."

"How'd you meet your partner?" Dan asked.

Goodman shrugged his shoulders and cut his gaze to Dan. "Met him online in a chat room. Let's just say I'm not the only one with this mission. You may have caught us, witch, but two more will take our place and we will wipe you and your kind from the face of the planet."

Charlie pursed her lips and did not take her eyes from his.

"How did you kill Ariel Martin and Chase Andrews?" Dan asked.

"You deaf or stupid? Like I said, with a good dose of their own damned medicine."

"What exactly did you give them?" Charlie asked.

"Just some herbs I grew in my back yard. Isn't that what y'all do? You grow your poisons in your gardens?"

"What did you give them?" Dan asked.

Goodman stared at her for a second more and then shifted his gaze to Dan. "A mix of deadly nightshade and hemlock. Mashed it up, soaked it in some hot water, and poured it down their gullets. I watched them until the light went out of their eyes and the devil took them to hell." The haughty expression on his face turned Charlie's stomach and she swallowed the bile rising in her throat.

Dan pushed a yellow notebook across the table with a pen. "I'm gonna need you to write that out. All of it. Including everything about your buddy and the name of the chat room."

"Fine. But I'm the one that gets the deal. Not him. You understand?"

"Oh, yeah," Charlie said rising to her feet. "I understand everything." She touched Dan's shoulder and left the room to meet with Ben.

CHARLIE AND BEN STOOD AT THE EDGE OF THE CUBICLES and watched while two deputies escorted Goodman from the interview room.

"Y'all take him over to booking," Dan said. "I'll be there shortly." He stopped and joined them, a smile on his face. "That was good work y'all. That fool didn't even ask what kind of deal he was gonna get."

"And you think his confession will hold up in court?" Ben asked.

"The DA will figure that out, but we've definitely got enough physical evidence from Chase's house to back it up. I'm gonna get a search warrant for Goodman's brother's house and if those plants are there like he said, that should seal the deal," Dan said.

"Good. And you'll let Juniper know?" Charlie asked.

"Of course," Dan said.

"Good." Charlie said. "Unless you need us, we're gonna take off."

"Can't blame you there but I'm gonna need a hug before you go." Dan opened his arms and Charlie embraced him, squeezing him tight. He let her go and looked into her eyes. "You know, I don't know how to thank you. This case would've gone cold if it weren't for you."

"You don't have to thank me. Just make sure it sticks. There's a decent sized witch population here and I want them to stay safe."

"Yeah," Dan said. "Me too."

"It's been a pleasure working with you," Ben said, and the two men shook hands. "If you ever need us..." Ben pulled his wallet from his front pocket and drew out a card. "Don't hesitate to call."

"Don't you worry." Dan gave the card a quick glance, then tucked it into his front breast pocket. He grinned. "I've got Charlie on speed dial for all things witchy. Y'all take care. I've gotta go see about a warrant."

"You too," Charlie said and the three of them walked to the front of the building together.

CHAPTER 31

"Come on, Mom, please?" Evan asked.

"I'm sorry, honey, but no," Charlie said.

"Please," Evan begged. "I'm sorry, okay? I swear I won't do it again."

"Evan, I said no, and I meant no. Do not ask me again." Charlie pulled into her driveway and maneuvered her Honda Civic around Will's Mustang and parked in the gravel space near her front porch. Evan pouted next to her. His bottom lip jutted out a little from the scowl marring his face.

"Ev—" She began, but he opened the door and got out without a word.

Charlie sighed and popped the trunk. Some days she just felt she could never get it right, even when her child had done something wrong. He grabbed his school bag out of the trunk and slammed the door shut before stalking up the steps. He stopped at the door to wait for her to catch up with the key.

Charlie climbed onto the porch and quickly unlocked the deadbolt. She'd adapted to using her hand with the cast and most of the pain had gone away.

"Don't you disappear. We've got to leave in about ten minutes for Uncle Jack's."

He grunted and went into his bedroom. The door slammed behind him, and she heard a thud.

"Sweet goddess give me strength," she muttered and put the mail she'd picked up on their way in on the large old trunk in front of her cushy, pale yellow couch. She moved into the kitchen and helped herself to a large glass of water. Since she'd started her energy healing work with Esperanza, she found herself constantly parched. Something moved at the corner of her eye. She fought the urge to jump and turn her head. Seeing shadows and flashes of light in her peripheral vision was another effect of her energy work. Some small part of her hoped it was a spirit or two, reaching out. Maybe in time she'd be able to look straight at them and ask them how she could help. Something touched her back and she jumped a little and turned to find Evan standing behind her.

"Oh, my goddess, Evan." She pressed one hand to her heart. "You scared the life out of me."

"Sorry. It's time to go," Evan said.

Charlie glanced at the clock on the wall. It read quarter past six. She took one last sip of water and poured the rest of it into the sink. She rinsed the glass and placed it upside down on the dishtowel.

"Do I have to go tonight? I'd rather just stay here."

"Yes, you do," she said, her patience wearing thin. This was new, Evan not wanting to join the family at Friday Night Dinner.

"Fine." He shrugged in a way that irritated her. "But if I can't have my phone, I'm not talking to anyone."

"Hey! You need to watch it. You hear me? You brought this punishment on yourself, young man. Skipping school with your girlfriend is not acceptable."

He rolled his eyes, made a face and walked away.

Is this what it was going to be like, raising a teenager? If so, goddess help the child because she wasn't sure she could keep her temper in check.

"Get your jacket, and let's go," Charlie said.

A moment later they walked out onto the porch and found Tom waiting for her at the bottom of the steps, a smile on his face. Tom waved. "Hey, Evan."

Evan didn't answer and instead ran ahead of them and was halfway across the yard before Charlie could stop him.

"I'm so sorry," Charlie said.

"He's mad now, but he'll get over it." Tom slipped his hand into hers and the two of them set off across the wide expanse of brown grass stretching between her small house and her uncle's. Jack's house glowed like a ghost beckoning to them in the evening light.

"Looks like a full house tonight," Charlie said, noting the number of cars in the driveway.

"Yep, and that's a good thing." Tom kissed her temple, and they made their way up the steps to the porch and through the back door.

"Hey, y'all." Charlie peeled off her black leather jacket and hung it up on one of the hooks near the door. Tom removed his gray coat and followed suit.

The comforting smell of chicken and biscuits permeated the air. Evangeline manned the stove where steam rose from two large pots. In one hand, she held a blue, quilted potholder, and in the other one, a large slotted spoon. At the kitchen table, Jen rolled out a round of dough, applying the full weight of her petite frame to get it as thin as possible. The remnants of two chicken carcasses rested on a sheet pan. The meat from the two chickens was piled high on another pan.

Lisa sat on the counter out of the way, hugging a small bowl to her chest and eating a baby carrot. She had braided her long hair to one side, and it fell down the front of her shoulder. "Hey, Charlie," she said.

"Hey. It smells divine in here. What are we having?" Charlie moved to the end of the kitchen table and rested her hands on the top of the chair.

"Chicken 'n dumplings." Jen picked up a pizza cutter and sliced uniform one-inch strips from the large square of thin dough. She picked up six strips and pivoted to the stove. Evangeline lifted the lid off the largest pot and stood back. Jen dropped the strips into the boiling broth, then cut and retrieved six more strips. Evangeline gently tamped down the dumplings but didn't stir. Jen cut strips from the rest of the dough and dropped them into the pot. Evangeline tamped those down, too, and then returned the pot lid.

"That should be enough to feed everyone," Evangeline said.

"I hope so." Jen brushed the flour off her hands over the sink and washed up quickly.

"Is there anything I can do?" Charlie asked. "Set the table?"

"Daphne already did it," Lisa said.

"I think we're good," Jen said and carefully folded up the waxed paper she'd placed underneath the dough.

Evangeline pulled two large pans of biscuits from the oven and set them on the counter.

"Charlie, could you put the biscuits in those two baskets?" Evangeline pointed to two stacked baskets lined with white linen napkins.

"Of course," Charlie said.

"I'm going to go say hi to everyone," Tom said.

"Okay," Charlie said.

"We're glad you're here, Tom," Evangeline said, giving him a smile.

"Thank you. I'm glad to be here." He disappeared through the doorway to the dining room and a few seconds later, she heard her uncle call, "Tom!" It sent a wave of gratitude flowing through her heart.

Charlie quickly washed her hands and began to pluck the hot biscuits one by one from the pans and place them carefully inside the baskets until the pans were empty. She pulled the corners of the napkins over the top of the biscuits to keep them warm.

Evangeline peeked inside the large pot. "The dumplings look done."

"Great," Jen said and began to add handfuls of chicken meat from the sheet pan into the pot.

"So, Charlie." Lisa bit into her carrot and crunched it. "Fill us in on what happened with your investigation."

"He turned out to be a good old-fashioned murderer. I talked to Dan this morning. They've already matched his DNA to one of the crime scenes and the DA is moving forward with first degree murder. The surprising part is that he wasn't really the mastermind. He had help. Someone working for the DOL."

"Yeah, Ben told me that," Jen said and slipped the hot lid back on the steaming pot.

"We still don't know how far reaching it is. The guy he gave up left the DOL six months ago and disappeared without a trace. One of my co-workers, you remember Athena? She found where our database had been hacked and tried to trace it but by the time we got agents there, he was gone."

"So, you think there are other people like him working for the DOL?" Lisa asked.

"We're still investigating. We found a chat room full of people claiming to be witchfinders making threats so we're looking into working with the FBI to trace them and determine if the threats are real or not," Charlie explained.

"That's terrible," Evangeline said.

"Hey, Charlie," a familiar voice called from the door. Charlie looked up to find Jason reaching into the bowl of carrots in Lisa's arms. He picked one from the top and took a bite. "How's your partner doing?"

"Will? He's still in a medically induced coma. He can only be in it for another week, and then some hard decisions will have to be made."

"Gosh, I can't even imagine," Jen said.

"Yeah," Charlie said.

"So how long till we eat?" Jason asked. Lisa gave him a dirty look.

"What?" he said with an innocent look to go along with his victim-shrug.

She shook her head and rolled her eyes.

"We should be ready to go in just a few minutes," Jen

said. "Charlie, would you take the biscuits into the dining room and put them on the table?"

"Of course," Charlie said. She picked up the two baskets and headed into the dining room. Jason pushed off from the counter and followed her.

"So, Lisa told me about the whole energy healing thing, and I just wanted to say I hope it works out for you," Jason said.

"I really appreciate that," she said and placed the baskets on the table. "It's already starting to work I think."

"Great, I've got a bunch of cases I could sure use your help with," he teased.

"Of course, you do." Charlie rolled her eyes.

"Just kidding. I just want you to be happy again and not avoid me anymore," he said.

"Who says I won't keep avoiding you?" she taunted. He made a hurt face. "I'm just joking."

"You better be," he said.

"Come on. Let's go round up the troops. Chicken 'n dumplings is my second favorite food on the planet, and I can't wait to dig in."

* * *

THE VAMPIRE HID AT THE EDGE OF THE WOODS AND watched curiously as the witch's son ran across the yard, leaving his mother and the reaper behind. He fingered the vial of dust and herbs in his pocket—the spell he'd gotten from the witch. The spell that would separate the reaper from his weapon and banish him from the presence of his love. His mouth watered at the thought of tasting Charlie Payne's blood.

The vampire stayed on his low perch unaffected by fatigue or even impatience. He settled in place to watch the back porch of the witch's house. In his three hundred years as a vampire, waiting had become his favorite game. Waiting and fantasizing about what he would do with his victims once he set his sights on a human. It had been a long time since he'd tasted the blood of a witch. A smile crept across his face. His mouth watered again, and he could barely contain his excitement. As soon as he had his fill of her blood and absorbed all her secrets, he would kill her and her entire family just as she had killed his.

CHAPTER 32

"Uncle Jack, do you have any chores I can do around here?" Evan asked before dragging his spoon across the melting vanilla ice cream and warm apple crisp on his plate.

"Maybe. What'd you have in mind?"

"I could mow the lawn or help you clean out the shed."

Jack Holloway put his spoon down, folded his hands together, and rested his chin on top of his knuckles. His crystal blue eyes narrowed, and the corners of his mouth drew up, noticeably raising his salt and pepper beard.

"And what exactly are you wanting to get out of this sudden interest in chores?"

Evan ignored the death glare from his mother. "Sir?"

"I'm assuming you aren't offering your services up for free. What are you looking for?"

"Evan." His mother's voice was full of warning.

"Free's fine. Anything to get me out of the house this weekend," Evan said.

"Evan," his mother said, her voice sterner than before. Evan glanced into her face and she mouthed the word, 'no.'

"Uncle Jack, I'm sorry, but Evan is on restriction for the next two weeks. So, he's not allowed to leave the house unless he's with me," Charlie said. Evan noticed her red cheeks. Was she mad or embarrassed?

"Nothing to be sorry about. The grass won't need mowing again till spring, but that's too bad because there's definitely chores I can have him help me with. Chores always used to make restriction fun for you girls, back in the day, didn't it?" Jack grinned.

"Oh yeah," Lisa said. "Fun, fun, fun."

His mother glared across the table at him. "You know, on second thought, maybe a few chores would be a good thing."

Evan ignored his mother.

Uncle Jack smirked. "See, now you're getting the hang of parenting a teenager."

"What would you like him to help you with first?" she asked.

"I've been meaning to sharpen the mower blades and

clean up my tools. He's old enough to help with that. Then maybe he can help me change the oil in Jen's truck."

"I think that's a fine idea," Charlie said. "What time do you want him here tomorrow?"

"Seven o'clock should be good," Jack said.

Evan sank down in his chair and pushed the rest of his dessert away. His cousin Jen sat next to him and nudged his elbow with hers. "You don't like the apple crisp?"

"It's good, I'm just not hungry anymore," Evan said. "May I be excused?"

"Yes, you may. Take your dish and put it by the sink please," his mother said.

Ruby, Jen's daughter, reached next to her big cousin for his plate. "Can I have it, Mama? Evan doesn't want his dessert."

Jen grabbed her little girl's hand and kissed it. "One dessert is enough for anybody, baby girl." Evan and Ruby gave each other commiserating looks.

Evan pushed away from the table and carried the half-eaten bowl of ice cream and apple crisp to the kitchen. He scooped up one last bite before he put it on the counter next to the stack of dishes to be washed.

That had not gone the way he had hoped. He wished his mother had not taken his phone, so he could go into the living room, ignore everyone and play video games until it was time to leave. He spotted his mother's bag peeking out from beneath her jacket. He glanced back at the dining room. He could get her keys, be across the yard and back before she even knew he was missing. She wouldn't even know he'd gotten his phone if he put it in his pocket and was careful not to let anyone see it.

Evan crossed the room, stopping to listen to the adults in the next room. They seemed embroiled in conversation. Good. He gingerly lifted his mother's bag from beneath her coat and dug through it until he found her keys. Then he crept outside onto the porch, being careful to close the back door as quietly as possible.

Once he was down the steps, he sprinted across the lawn separating his uncle's house from his mom's. A thrill of excitement went through him, and he imagined himself a bold adventurer. There was something exhilarating about stealing this little bit of freedom and doing things he'd never done alone before, like going into his mom's house without her. It was his house too, right? He lived there half the time. So, yeah, it wasn't like he was breaking the rules really.

He pushed the key into the lock and turned the deadbolt.

When he walked into the living room, every hair on his neck and arms stood at attention.

Something was wrong. He flipped on the light and

scanned the living room and what he could see of the kitchen/dining area. The rooms were empty.

A soft mewling sound came from his mother's bedroom.

"Poe?" Evan called. He headed to his mother's room and flipped on the light.

Meow. Meow. Meow.

The distressed sound of the cat tugged at his heart, but he didn't see her.

"Poe? Where are you?" Evan knelt next to the bed and peered beneath it. The six-month-old kitten was huddled under the bed. Evan appraised the situation. The kitten had pushed herself against the wall, dead center of his mother's queen-sized headboard. It would take some maneuvering to get her out without moving all the furniture around. Something his mother would surely notice. A blast of cold air sent a shiver down his spine, and he popped up to his knees to look for the source. It was too cold for the windows to be open. When his gaze found the doorway, his heart beat its way up his throat at the sight of the apparition of a woman standing just outside his mother's bedroom. "Get under the bed," she hissed. "He's coming."

The door slammed shut, and he heard a lock click.

Evan got to his feet and ran to the door. His hands wrapped around the knob and twisted it back and forth while he pulled. The door wouldn't budge. Panic fluttered in his chest and traveled up his neck, threatening to choke him.

"Open the door!" He banged on the back of the door. A loud knocking from the other side shook the door, and Evan startled. He stepped back to come up with a plan. His heart hammered in his ears, but it wasn't enough to drown out the loud rhythmic banging from the other side.

He looked around, trying to suss out the best place to hide. The iPad on his mother's nightstand sitting among a litter of crystals and books caught his attention. He could text her. The knocking became louder, spurring him to grab the tablet and dive under the bed with the kitten.

He swiped the tablet to life and quickly jotted off a group text to his mother's phone, Jen's phone, Lisa's phone, Daphne's phone, and even his Aunt Evangeline's phone, just in case old ladies texted.

Please come quick. There's a ghost in the house with me.

The knocking stopped, and Evan held his breath. He watched the screen for any sign she'd gotten the text. He wished he could see the door, but his view of it was blocked from his spot under the bed. Somehow no knocking was worse than the knocking had been. At least he'd known where the spirit was while she knocked.

Where R you? We've been looking all over for you.

At home. Under ur bed.

Hold tight, we're coming.

The sound of the lock clicking and the doorknob turning resounded across the room. Something warm moved close to him. The kitten rubbed up against his cheek, taking up residence between him and the door. He felt the cat's black fur rise across her back, and a soft hiss escape her. The door hinge squealed a little when the door opened a few inches. A growl started deep inside the kitten's chest. Evan blinked when he saw feet. Solid and not shadowy, black heavy-soled boots clomped across the floor toward the bed. He squeezed his eyes shut. The air around him grew very cold, and Poe hissed and growled louder.

Please, oh please, Mom, hurry up.

He wished he knew a spell to make himself invisible. Did that even exist? The man's feet moved to the closet first, and he heard the door open. Evan peeked through one eye and watched the man rifle through his mother's clothes. The man stopped and Evan could hear him breathing in deeply and blowing it out loudly.

"I can smell you, witch boy. Your blood smells as sweet as your mother's." He laughed a husky laugh and knelt next to the end of the bed. Evan opened his mouth to scream but choked. Time seemed to slow down. The quilt lifted and a pallid man with dark red circles beneath his bloodshot eyes appeared. His lips twisted into a leering grin and his black eyes glittered in the light.

"There you are," he purred. He grinned, baring shiny

jagged teeth. Evan's throat finally opened, and a guttural scream lifted from his belly, through his chest and out of his mouth. "Yes. Yes! Scream, boy. Scream so she hears you." The man grabbed Evan's ankle and yanked him hard, pulling him from beneath the bed in one motion.

"My mother is on her way! She'll be walking into the house any minute."

"Good, good." The man chuckled. "Let her come."

A large amethyst crystal flew across the room and struck the man in the temple. Evan saw the spirit girl appear.

"What the hell?" he muttered and touched the spot where the hard rock had hit him. He looked down at his fingertips and rubbed them together, smearing the blood coating them. He gritted his teeth and stared down at Evan. "Did you do that, boy?"

"What? No. She did it." He pointed to the girl, but she disappeared in a flash.

The jewelry box on his mother's dresser flew open, and two more crystals sailed across the room, aimed at the man. He saw them coming and ducked before they could hit him.

The front door opened, and the sound of footsteps filled Evan's senses and his heart with hope. *His mother was here! She would save him!*

The man grabbed him by the throat and lifted him

into the air as if he weighed nothing. Evan clawed at the man's wrists and struggled to breathe.

"Put him down, vampire," his mother said, pointing her wand at him. The man pivoted, putting Evan between himself and his mother. His cousins, his great aunt, and his mother's boss Ben gathered behind her with their wands drawn.

Tom pushed his way to the front. "It's going to be all right, Evan," he said. "Stay calm." Tom's face and body transformed into the stuff of his nightmares. A faceless grim reaper, with flowing robes and a scythe with a dark curved metal blade in one skeletal hand. Evan let out a garbled scream, and everything grew gray at the corners of his vision, then went dark.

* * *

"Dammit." The vampire grunted and dropped Evan in front of him in a heap. Charlie let off a stunning shot at the creature with her wand, but it seemed not to affect him. Tom floated ahead of the witches. He darted left, a blur of black and then darted right. The vampire kept his focus on the reaper's movements.

"Brother and sister, I need you," Tom said softly. Within a few seconds, two more reapers appeared, their scythes in hand.

"A whole reaper clan," the vampire mused. "How wonderful."

The three reapers circled the vampire, their scythes drawn back as if they were ready to cut him down at any second.

The vampire grabbed Evan again, this time by his ankle and hoisted him into the air in front of him like a shield. Charlie and her cousins formed a line.

"Be careful of Evan," Charlie said, and took aim looking for the first available opportunity to stun the vampire long enough so Tom could behead him.

The vampire laughed and drew something from the pocket inside his coat. He held it out and spoke with conviction.

"Reaper, reaper deathly fright,
Reaper, reaper be gone from my sight."

The vampire threw the vial in his hand onto the hardwood floor with such force the glass exploded. A silvery dust blew outward, and one by one, two of the reapers disappeared. Tom rushed forward, with his scythe swung back to serve up a death blow but he disappeared within a foot of the vampire. His scythe fell to the floor with a clatter. The vampire let out a giddy laugh.

"I can't believe that worked! Now I really am grateful I didn't kill that old witch," he crowed. He kicked Tom's weapon across the floor.

Charlie raised her wand. "Aim for his chest and his

head and repeat after me: *With this light, I stun thee into stillness, where you can do no harm."* Her cousins repeated her words.

The tips of their wands glowed with blue energy. They each got off a round of shots of the stunning energy before he lifted the boy higher. The spells hit Evan instead of the vampire.

"Stop!" Charlie held up her hand. They all paused their shots, but the tips of their wands still glowed with power, ready to shoot. "Let my son go, and I will go with you."

"No, Charlie," Lisa shouted.

"Charlie." Jen gasped.

"Charlie, what are you doing?" Ben asked, his voice full of desperation.

Charlie threw a glance over her shoulder at him. "It's okay. I'll be okay. He can't hurt me, remember?" she whispered.

"Charlie, wait. I don't know that it will still work," Ben said.

Charlie choked back tears "It has to. It's the only way."

"Charlie don't do this," Ben said.

Her voice shook. "It's gonna be just fine." Charlie forced herself to look away from her family. If she thought about it too much, she might lose her nerve. She dropped her wand on the ground and held up her hands in surrender. "Let him go. Now."

"Only if you and I can pass unscathed by them." The vampire gestured to her cousins.

"Fine. Y'all back away from the door," Charlie commanded.

One by one, Jen, Lisa, Daphne, Evangeline and Ben stepped aside giving the vampire a wide berth. Charlie stepped forward and met the vampire halfway. "Drop my son."

The vampire tossed Evan aside and he crumpled to the ground, motionless.

Jason stepped into the threshold of the house, with his weapon drawn and trained on the vampire's chest. "I've got a clean shot, Charlie."

"No!" Charlie stepped forward, blocking Jason.

The vampire reached for her; a look of victory etched into his features. "Don't worry. It will only hurt for a moment."

The second his icy cold hand touched her arm she felt an electric jolt sizzle through her body. The spell Ben cast might have weakened over the last couple of days but it had not completely faded.

The vampire's eyes widened, and the shock of Ben's spell sent him flying backward. He slammed against the wall dividing the living room and kitchen, slid to the floor, and for a short second, shook his head to get his bearings. He sprang to his feet growling and a rasping scream escaped his blood-colored lips before he charged her. A shot rang out behind her and Charlie felt the bullet whiz past, too close for comfort. It struck the vampire in the chest knocking him back a step. He slowed only for a second—just long enough for Charlie to pick up Tom's scythe from the floor. The handle thrummed in her hands, and she focused her energy on one thought. *Take his head.* And as if the scythe had no choice but to obey, it yanked her forward, and with strength she didn't know she possessed, she reared the weapon back and swung it in one smooth motion. The vampire's head came away from his body and he took a few more steps before he fell dead to the ground.

Charlie dropped the scythe on the floor and stared down at the vampire's corpse. "Holy shit." Her chest heaved. "He's dead."

"Will," Ben said.

Charlie met his eyes and she sprinted for the door, grabbing the keys to Will's car. When she returned with an empty syringe, she thrust it at Ben. He crossed to the vampire's body, plunged it into the dead creature's chest and drew it full of blood. "I've got to get this to the DOL hospital in Charlotte."

Charlie knelt next to her son alongside her aunt and cousins. "There's a cooler on top of the fridge. Empty the ice into it and put that inside," she said. She moved to cradle Evan's head. Ben nodded and disappeared into the kitchen.

Ben emerged with a cooler in hand. "I'll call y'all later."

"Come on Ben, I'll drive you," Jason offered.

"You sure?"

"Yeah. I can get us there faster. All I have to do is turn on my blue lights," Jason said.

"Great," Ben said and the two of them left the house.

Charlie gently stroked Evan's hair and watched her aunt make a quick evaluation.

"He's okay," Evangeline said, lifting his lids to look at his pupils. She cupped his cheek. "Just stunned, that's all. He should wake up soon."

Evan groaned and his eyes began to flutter.

"See?" Evangeline said. She patted his arm. "He's fine."

"Mom?" Evan said, his voice raspy.

"I'm here, baby. I'm here." She leaned down and kissed his forehead.

"There's a spirit in the house," he whispered.

"What?" Charlie asked.

"A spirit. Of a girl. She tried to save me." Evan turned his head toward the bedroom and pointed to the door. "There she is."

Charlie followed the line of his finger and her breath caught in her throat. A pale apparition of a young woman stood in the doorway. Tears stung her eyes.

"Ariel?"

The young woman smiled and nodded. "Thank you, Charlie, for all that you did for us."

Hot tears spilled onto Charlie's cheeks. A flickering shadow appeared next to Ariel and came into focus. Chase Andrews's spirit.

"Hi Charlie," he said. "I'm glad you got my message."

Charlie sniffled and let out a nervous little laugh. "Hi Chase," she whispered. "A fat lot of good it did you."

"You stopped him. That's all that matters."

"Yes. That's all that matters," Ariel said.

"Do you need help crossing over?" Charlie asked.

The two apparitions joined hands and smiled. "No, we can find the way. Take care of yourself. And keep your eyes open. There are more like Goodman out there."

"I know," Charlie said.

"Charlie?" Evangeline asked. "Are you okay?"

"What?" Charlie shifted her gaze to her aunt's concerned face.

"You spaced out there for a minute and you're crying. Are you okay?" Evangeline asked.

Charlie glanced at the threshold to her bedroom and the spirits were gone. A grin pulled at her lips. "I'm fine," she said and let out a laugh. "I'm better than fine."

CHAPTER 33

Charlie put the plastic bowl of chicken 'n dumplings into the microwave and pressed the options for Thaw. Evan sat at the little bistro table in her kitchen, doing his homework.

"Dinner will be ready soon," she said.

"What are we having?" he asked, looking up from his work.

"I thought we'd have the chicken 'n dumplings Jen put in the freezer for us last month," Charlie said.

Evan shivered. "Can't we just have pizza?"

Charlie sighed and pulled a pizza from the freezer. "Sure, honey." She stripped it out of its plastic wrapper and turned on the oven. A moment later, she placed the frozen circle on a pan and put it inside to bake.

"So, you don't like chicken 'n dumplings anymore?" Charlie asked.

"No, thank you," he muttered. "Reminds me too much of vampires."

A knock on the door drew her attention, and she ruffled his sandy hair as she left the kitchen.

She crossed the living room. She finally had stopped looking down at the place where the vampire had died and bled all over her rug. Tom, Jen and Ben had helped her roll up the inexpensive Berber carpet remnant, and her uncle had towed it to the dump.

Charlie opened the door to find Will Tucker on her porch. She pushed open the screen door. "Will! Come on in. When did you get out of the hospital?"

"They let me out this morning." He stepped inside, looked toward Evan, and waved. Evan stared at him, a curious look on his face.

"Evan, go wash up for dinner please and clear your books off the table. Okay?"

"Sure." He closed his books and shoved them into his book bag before he set off for the bathroom.

"I just wanted to swing by and get the keys to my car. If that's okay," he said.

"Of course, it's okay. It's your car. Although, I will say, my son has been eyeing it for the last month."

"I appreciate you taking care of it for me," he said.

"You're welcome. I'm glad I can give it back to you."

She reached for the keys hanging from one of the hooks next to the door and handed it to him.

"I never did thank you for saving my life. For not giving up," Will said.

"You don't have to thank me. I'd like to think you'd do the same thing for me." She folded her arms across her chest easily now with her cast finally off.

Will nodded and fiddled with the keys in his hands. "So, I'll be back at work on Monday."

"Great. I've missed working with you. And we've got a ton of cases, so having you back will be fantastic."

"I look forward to it. And you know what I really want to hear about?" Will asked.

"What?" Charlie grinned.

"I want to hear the whole bloody story about how you chopped that SOB's head off."

Evan emerged from the bathroom. He gave them a wary glance.

"Well, I better go so y'all can eat your dinner," he said.

"You're welcome to stay," she said. "I've got plenty."

"Thanks, I appreciate that, but I'm eating with Ben and Jen tonight."

"All right," she said. "We'll talk more next week."

"You bet," he said.

Charlie watched him walk across the yard and ascend the steps to her uncle's house before she closed the door.

"Come on, Mom, the pizza's ready, I think."

"Well, take it out of the oven. If you're old enough to skip school, you're old enough to take a pan out of the oven," she teased.

"Geez, you are never gonna let me live that down, are you?"

"Nope," she said, joining him in the kitchen. He'd already pulled the pan out of the oven and put it on the stove. She put her arm around his shoulders and hugged him to her.

"So, do you think Will would teach me how to fight vampires?"

Charlie chuckled and kissed her son on the cheek. "No way. You being a witch is enough."

THANK YOU FOR READING *BAD OMENS*. THIS WAS SUCH A fun book to write. I've wanted to introduce vampires for a while, and this was the perfect outlet. Although my favorite part of writing this book was writing about Charlie's journey back to herself after her near-death experience.

In the next book, *Enduring Spirits* Charlie is still working on healing her energy and at times must handle all the chaos it can bring, including a flood of ghosts vying for her attention. There will be lots of mystery, magic, ghostly encounters and family time to keep you entertained.

Click here to get your copy of Enduring Spirits.

Connect with me

One of the things I love most about writing is building a relationship with my readers. We can connect in several different ways.

Join my reader's newsletter.

By signing up for my monthly newsletter, you will get information on preorders, new releases and exclusive content just for my reader's newsletter. You can join by clicking here: https://wendy-wang-books.ck. page/482af1c7a3

You can also follow me on my Amazon page if you prefer not to get another email in your inbox. Follow me here.

Connect with me on Facebook

Want to comment on your favorite scene? Or make suggestions for a funny ghostly encounter for Charlie? Or tell me what sort of magic you'd like to see Jen, Daphne and Lisa perform? Like my Facebook page and let me know. I post content there regularly and talk with my readers every day.

FACEBOOK: HTTPS://WWW. facebook.com/wendywangauthor

LET'S TALK ABOUT OUR FAVORITE BOOKS IN MY READERS group on Facebook.

Readers Group: https://www.facebook.com/groups/1287348628022940/ ;

YOU CAN ALWAYS DROP ME AN EMAIL. I LOVE TO HEAR FROM my readers

Email: http://www.wendywangbooks.com/contact.html

THANK YOU AGAIN FOR READING!

Printed in Great Britain
by Amazon

28716745R00180